Long Road Home

Praise for Maya Banks's
Long Road Home

"The plot of Long Road Home is fraught with more twists and bumps than the Titan roller coaster at Six Flags over Texas!"

~ *2k2s Kwips and Kritiques*

"Readers, take a long deep breath because once you dive into Long Road Home you will be constantly sitting on the edge of your seat sharply inhaling as you move from one exciting, thrilling scene into the very next."

~ *Fallen Angel Reviews*

"I found myself totally immersed in the story and unable to put it down. ...Long Road Home was simply magnificent."

~ *Joyfully Reviewed*

Look for these titles by
Maya Banks

Long Road Home

Maya Banks

SAMHAIN
PUBLISHING

Samhain Publishing, Ltd.
11821 Mason Montgomery Rd., 4B
Cincinnati, OH 45249
www.samhainpublishing.com

Long Road Home
Copyright © 2011 by Maya Banks
Second Print ISBN: 978-1-60928-302-5
First Print ISBN: 978-1-59998-962-4
Second Digital ISBN: 978-1-60928-300-1
First Digital ISBN: 978-1-59998-618-0

Editing by Jennifer Miller
Cover by Mandy M. Roth

This book was previously published under the name of Sharon Long. It has been revised and rewritten for the 2011 release.
First Samhain Publishing, Ltd. electronic publication: November 2007
Second Samhain Publishing, Ltd. electronic publication: August 2011
First Samhain Publishing, Ltd. print publication: August 2008
Second Samhain Publishing, Ltd. print publication: August 2011

Dedication

To Jess Bimberg for giving me my start with Samhain. I so appreciate everything you did for me and will always be grateful that you wanted to publish that first book, and especially Colters' Woman. You were such a key factor at the beginning of my career.

And to Jennifer Miller for always going the extra mile to make my stories awesome. It's been wonderful to work with you and I'll miss you and your thorough editorial. I've learned so much from you. We've had such a great run!

Finally to all the readers who've supported me from the very beginning of my career. You've made all of my success possible. I wouldn't have been able to do it without you. Thank you.

Chapter One

Jules Trehan climbed out of her rented Jeep and looked warily around her. The remote cabin she had been staying in for the last week had afforded her privacy...so far. But she didn't harbor any illusions that it would last for long. Northstar would find her. It was time to leave.

She slammed the door and leaned heavily on the cold metal. Around her, the rugged beauty of the mountains gave her a small measure of comfort she'd long been without. Sadness that she would soon move on crept through her, inserting an unrelenting ache in her chest.

Closing her eyes, she breathed deeply of the pine-scented air. Here in this untamed land, the illusion of freedom was ever present, yet she viewed it as she would a magician's feat— pleasing, but not real.

Though she knew she must hurry, she allowed herself one more moment to revel in the stark beauty of the Colorado sky. Regret. So much regret. She closed her eyes and then deliberately hardened her mind, shutting out everything but the task at hand. *Survival.*

Spurred to action, she mounted the steps to the cabin that overlooked Miramonte Reservoir and opened the door. She slipped inside, intent on collecting her sparse belongings and hitting the road.

There wasn't much to pack. She threw a change of clothes and several packets of dried rations into an overnight bag. All her weapons, with the exception of the pistol she carried, were secured in the back of the Jeep, and the rest of her supplies were tucked away in a locker in Denver. She'd go there next to collect them. Then she'd disappear to some foreign country and start a new life. And if she were really lucky, she could escape the person she had become.

The sound of tires crunching on gravel drew her attention to the window. She yanked her gun from her back waistband and hurried in the direction of the door. She flattened herself against the wall next to the window, and, with one finger, she pulled the curtains slightly open and peered out. A light-colored sedan pulled to a stop beside her Jeep.

She gripped the stock of her pistol, and her finger caressed the trigger. Adrenaline pumped furiously through her veins as she waited for the occupants to get out. When they did, she nearly dropped the gun in shock. Pain, and so much longing, throbbed through her veins. How had Mom and Pop found her?

She jerked away from the window and leaned her head against the wall. It was a trick. It had to be. Look-alikes hired by Northstar.

Footsteps sounded on the steps, and she slid over to the door, her gun raised. Her breath came in rapid spurts as her throat swelled with unspent sobs.

A soft knock pierced the quiet. "Jules?" Her mother's wavering voice drifted through the heavy wooden door.

God, it sounded just like her mom. Fear gripped her. Had the Trehans been harmed? Had Northstar carried out his threats?

She cracked the door and shoved her gun out at the older couple. "Who are you? What do you want?"

"Put that damn thing away," Marshall Trehan groused. "Is that any way to greet us after three years?"

She thrust her gun back into her pants and threw open the door. She was in her mother's arms in an instant.

"Jules, my God, it's really you." Her mother's arms tightened around her.

Jules closed her eyes and inhaled the comforting scent of her mom. Still a mixture of vanilla and butter after all these years.

"Do you have a hug for your old man?"

She released her mother and went willingly into Pop's arms. His strong embrace seemed weaker than usual, but he still smelled of Old Spice aftershave. He patted her on the back and kissed the top of her head. "You've got a lot of explaining to do, girl."

Reality quickly tempered her euphoria. She drew away and gestured her parents inside. As they walked by, she scanned the outside perimeter, taking in every detail of her surroundings.

At her side, her phone pulsed and vibrated. Dread stole over her.

"I'll be right back in, Pop."

"Be quick. You don't want to keep your mother waiting," he said gruffly.

She closed the door behind her and yanked out her phone. "What do you want?" She walked toward her Jeep as she waited for a response.

"Always to the point. I admire that about you."

"Try it sometime," she bit out.

"Enjoying your visit with the Trehans?"

She froze. "Are you behind this?"

"I would think you'd appreciate it."

She remained silent, her mind working quickly. Northstar did nothing that didn't benefit him.

"Why?" she asked.

"It's simple, Magalie. I want you back."

"My name is Jules," she ground out.

"What you call yourself is inconsequential. I want to bring you back in. I know where you are. Your pitiful attempts at hiding are no credit to your training. I let you have a little vacation. It's time to get back to work."

"No."

"What?"

"I said no."

"I really hoped you wouldn't say that," he said in a regretful tone. "It's a shame the Trehans traveled all this way for nothing."

She dropped the phone and started for the cabin in a full sprint. "Mom, Pop!" she screamed.

She was almost to the porch when the entire world exploded around her. A ball of fire flashed in her vision as a violent force propelled her backwards, her body arcing in the air.

She slammed viciously to the ground, wood and debris raining down on her like a hailstorm. Pain racked her entire body, and her vision blurred, the sky swirling above her.

Tears slipped down her cheeks. "Mom, Pop," she croaked out.

Then everything went black.

Chapter Two

Montrose, Colorado

Manuel Ramirez stepped off the plane, slinging his carry-on over his shoulder. He walked briskly past the security checkpoints, noting the lines of people waiting to pass through. Tourist season was in full swing. His partner had arranged for a car, and hopefully he would breeze right through and be on his way. To see Jules.

For three years he'd looked for her. Utilizing every connection and department resource in his power, he'd left no stone unturned in his urgency to discover why she had disappeared. But even his position with the CIA hadn't helped him in his quest.

Then, as suddenly as she had fallen off the face of the earth she'd reappeared. He'd dropped everything and flown to Colorado, praying that it wasn't yet another dead end in a long line of disappointments.

He collected the necessary paperwork from the car rental counter and headed outside, anxious to begin the drive to Norwood.

His chest tightened as he imagined seeing Jules for the first time in three years. Was she okay? Had she been hurt? Thousands of questions burned a trail through his head.

Through countless missions in the last few years, his number one thought had been of her. If she was hungry, hurting, alone, scared. Trips home had become more difficult as he had to face the Trehans each time with no answers to their questions. Watching them slowly sink further into despair and into the belief that their adopted daughter was dead had been more than he could bear.

How would she react to seeing him? If she was in Norwood, why hadn't she called him? Why the silence? Why had she *never* called him?

He shook his head as he climbed into the car. So many questions and no real answers. Not yet anyway.

As he started the engine, his cell phone rang. He answered, knowing it was Tony. "Talk to me."

A long period of silence followed. "Manuel."

"What is it?"

"I don't know how to say this, man." Tony's voice was heavy with sadness, and Manuel's pulse immediately began to race. "It's the Trehans."

"Mom and Pop?" Manuel relaxed. "Did they call? You didn't tell them about Jules, did you? I don't want to get their hopes up if this turns out to be a dead end."

"Manuel, they were there."

His brow wrinkled in confusion. "Where?"

Tony sighed. "They went to Jules's cabin in Norwood. I don't know how they found out she was there. Maybe she called them."

"No, they would've let me know." But they hadn't let him know they were going, had they? Why? He blew out his breath. "How'd they find out where she was?"

"Manuel, there's more."

Dread gripped him as he waited for Tony to continue.

"There was an explosion. The entire cabin blew up. The Trehans were inside."

"What?" It couldn't be true. There had to be some mistake. Then another thought hit him. "Jules?" he demanded, barely able to croak out her name. "What about Jules?"

"She's alive."

Relief poured over him, making him lightheaded and dizzy. She was all he had left now. He couldn't lose her.

"She's in the hospital in Grand Junction. She was airlifted from Norwood."

"How bad is it?"

"I don't know, man. She's alive. That's all I know. You need to get to Grand Junction fast. I don't know what's going on, but I'm working on this end to try and figure it out. Your girl has some nasty enemies, and she isn't safe. Sanderson and I are working on a transfer as soon as she's stable."

"Thanks, Tony," he whispered. "Tell the boss man I appreciate his help."

"There's one other thing, Manny," Tony said, slipping to the nickname only Jules used.

Manuel waited as he heard Tony shuffling through papers, the crackling coming over the receiver. He heard someone else in the background. Sanderson?

Tony's voice came back over the phone. "There was a veritable arsenal in Jules's Jeep. High-tech stuff. Not the run-of-the-mill self-defense for the average citizen. Most of it's Russian. Sanderson thinks your girl is in quite a bit of trouble."

Manuel closed his eyes and shook his head in an effort to dispel the overwhelming confusion. Guns? Jules? What the fuck? "I'll call you when I get to Grand Junction." He tossed the phone onto the seat and tried to steady himself. His hands shook, and he curled his fingers into fists.

Jules was alive, a fact that gave him unending joy. But the people who'd been such an important factor in his life were dead. He'd entered their lives when he was ten years old. An angry, sullen little boy whose mother had flitted in and out of his world when it suited her mood. He'd crept over to their house when things at his own home had gotten unbearable. They'd represented the only semblance of normalcy he'd had in his young life.

And now they were gone. Raw pain twisted in his chest. His hands clenched the steering wheel, and he gritted his teeth in anger. Whoever had done this to Jules—to his family—was going to pay.

Chapter Three

Grand Junction, Colorado

Jules became aware of horrific pain, and her first thought was that she couldn't possibly be dead and feel so much hurt. She pried her eyes open and winced when white, hot light poured into her vision. Her eyes slammed shut once more.

She lay still, trying to take stock of her situation. The smell told her she was in a hospital. That nauseating, sterile odor could only come from a medical setting. Her head pounded, and her chest was on fire.

Her nose felt dry and raw. Then she realized it was because oxygen blew a steady stream into her nostrils. She attempted to open her eyes again, squinting against the inevitable onslaught of light.

A blurred figure stood at the foot of her bed. She blinked a few times, wincing at the pain that shot through her head with the slight movement.

As the figure came into focus, her heart constricted, robbing her of precious breath. *Manny.* Even with his back to her, she recognized him instantly. She swallowed hard, trying desperately to rid herself of the knot in her throat.

He was big. Much bigger than she remembered. His well-muscled arms strained at the sleeves of the polo shirt he wore. Dark slacks molded solid thighs. He towered over the bed, filling the room with his indomitable presence. And suddenly she was afraid.

She closed her eyes again, not wanting to alert him to the fact she was awake. He would hate her for what she'd done.

Mom and Pop. God. She choked as the knot grew larger in her throat. She took several deep gulps of air in through her nose, praying the oxygen did its job.

Full-scale panic threatened to overcome her. She'd killed her parents. People Manny loved dearly. She'd sworn that she'd never allow them to come to harm. It was why she had stayed away for three long years. And now her worst fears had been realized. All because she'd called Northstar's bluff. And lost.

If Manny found out, he would despise her. The Trehans were everything to him. How could she live with herself after what she'd done? How could she have hurt everyone she ever loved?

Pain flashed through her head, and nausea rolled in her stomach. The explosion registered in her mind over and over. She opened her eyes in an attempt to make it all go away.

A ragged moan tore from her lips before she could call it back.

Manny jerked around, concern etched in every facet of his face. "Jules!" He rushed to her side, his hand reaching out to touch her cheek. "Are you in pain?"

She squeezed her eyes shut, weakened by the joy that flooded through her at the sound of his voice.

His rough thumb smoothed gently over her cheek. "Should I call the nurse?"

Her eyes fluttered open again. "No," she croaked. She swallowed and tried to speak. For a long moment, she stared into his familiar green eyes. Love and concern, two things she was unworthy of, reflected in their depths.

He left her side and poured water from the pitcher by the sink into a plastic cup. Returning, he held the cup to her lips. She sipped gratefully at the cool liquid, a soothing balm to her raw throat.

When she was finished, he set the cup aside and pulled a chair up to the bed. He settled down and curled his warm hand around her limp one. Heat spread comfortingly up her arm.

He picked up her hand and kissed it. "Thank God you're alive."

She choked as a sob mounted. She breathed frantically, willing her iron control not to desert her. It was too much. Her lips slipped open, and a raw sound of agony burst from her chest.

Her breaths came jerkily and tears burned a fiery trail down her cheeks. "I'm so sorry."

"What are you sorry for, baby?" His worried gaze swept over her.

She took in a huge breath. "Mom, Pop."

Pain contorted his brow. He glanced briefly away as if to compose himself. When he looked back at her, only his eyes held a shadow of sadness. "Try not to think about that now," he murmured. "You need to rest and get better so I can take you home."

Home. The word sent shards of pain racing through her. She no longer had a home. No longer had a family. Manny was all she had left, and he would die just like the Trehans.

His hand cupped her cheek, soothing the hurt away with gentle fingers. What she wouldn't give to let him solve all her problems, just like she had done so many times in her youth.

He had always been there when she had fallen, her protector. Only now, she had to be the one to protect him.

She inhaled deeply, allowing his spicy scent to curl over her. It provided her comfort, if only for a few moments. He leaned forward, pressing his lips to her forehead as his hand stroked her hair. "Do you hurt? Do I need to call the nurse?"

She hurt all over, but even the strongest narcotic wasn't going to take away her pain. And she couldn't allow her mind to be dulled. She was a sitting duck in this hospital, both she and Manny targets.

Slowly, she shook her head. "I'm okay."

Manuel watched the battle play out over her face, his gut clenching at her obvious pain. Her injuries weren't life-threatening, thank God, but her ribs had taken a hell of a beating.

He had to work to keep his hands off her. He needed to touch her, hold her. Convince himself that she was lying here in front of him, very much alive. In his darkest hours, he'd allowed himself a brief moment to believe that she really might be dead. Might never come back. Yet here she was. Changed. Very different from the starry-eyed girl who had left for France three years ago. But still, it was her. What horrors had she endured?

He tamped down the surge of impatience. His questions could be answered later. For now he would rejoice in the fact that she had come back to him, and he would see to her safety. He stood up and squeezed her hand. "Get some rest. I'll be close by."

Her eyelids were already fluttering closed as he stepped into the hall. He pulled out his phone and punched in Tony's number.

"How is she?" Tony asked immediately as he answered.

Manuel sighed. How to answer that question? She was alive, but beyond that he wasn't sure *how* she was at all. "She's okay, I think."

"I've arranged her transfer to a military hospital in Bethesda. The paperwork is materializing as we speak. She'll be transported to the airport by ambulance. An army helicopter will fly her to the base in Colorado Springs. From there, she'll be flown to Maryland."

"Thanks, Tony. I owe you."

"Not a problem. Even the army won't have a clue who she is." Tony chuckled.

"You find anything else out?" Manuel asked after a moment's hesitation.

"Not yet, but I'm on it."

Manuel hung up the phone. Tony would come through. There wasn't much he couldn't find out. Being a computer geek for the CIA had its perks.

He re-entered Jules's room but stood quietly back, watching her sleep. Her pale face held such an air of vulnerability. A wave of possessiveness rolled over him, startling him with its ferocity. Though her adopted parents had played an important role in his life, his feelings for her were not those of a sibling. They never had been.

He moved quietly back to her bedside and eased into the chair by her head. To his surprise, she opened her eyes. Those beautiful blue eyes that had haunted his dreams for so long.

"You should be asleep," he said reproachfully. Unable to help himself, he smoothed a short blonde curl from her forehead and tucked it behind her ear. She'd cut her hair.

Her expression was inscrutable. "When can I get out of here?"

He arched an eyebrow. "You'll be leaving in a few hours, but don't get any ideas. I'm having you transferred to a hospital in Maryland where I can keep a close eye on you."

She frowned. "Maryland?"

"I'll explain everything later. When you're better." Though how he was going to explain his other life to her, he didn't know.

"Do you live in Maryland now?"

"You could say that," he said vaguely.

"I don't have any clothes," she said with a frown. "I can't go anywhere. Can you go out and get me something? Please? I'll pay you back, I promise."

"For God's sake, Jules. Don't worry about paying me back. But I shouldn't leave you alone."

She shrugged. "I'm sure your watchdogs won't let anything happen to me."

He stared at her in surprise. How had she known about the guards he had posted? An uneasy feeling stole over him before he shook it off. This was Jules. And all she wanted was something to wear. "I'll be back in less than an hour. While I'm gone I want you to sleep."

She nodded tiredly and sank further into her pillows. Dropping a kiss on her head, he turned and walked out the door. He informed the two guards of his plans and gave them strict instructions not to allow anyone but the doctor and nurse inside the room.

His feeling of unease followed him out of the hospital. Leaving Jules wasn't his most brilliant idea. He paused for a moment when he got to his car. Glancing toward the entrance, he considered going back. He could always get her clothes later.

They weren't important. Her safety was. Digging out his phone, he dialed Tony again.

"Speak to me," Tony said.

"How are you at picking out women's clothing?"

Tony chuckled. "I haven't had any complaints. You thinking of a wardrobe change?"

"Not for me, bonehead. Jules. She wants some clothes, and I don't feel comfortable leaving her alone."

"I'll take care of it, but you owe me big-time, buddy. Buying women's clothing isn't my thing. Now if you wanted something from Victoria's Secret, I'm your man, but somehow I don't see you wanting a teddy for Jules."

Manuel rolled his eyes. "Just get her the basics. I'll make it up to you."

"Damn right you will."

As Tony hung up, Manuel grinned. He could protest all he wanted, but Tony would do just about anything for him. A sentiment Manuel returned.

Feeling better, he strode back into the hospital. He stopped briefly by the cafeteria and bought a cup of coffee. He hadn't had any in over twenty-four hours, and he was feeling it. He took a cautious sip as he stepped into the elevator. It was terrible. Had the consistency of motor oil. But it was caffeine and it smelled like coffee, so he didn't complain.

When he arrived at Jules's door, he nodded to the guards and quietly walked inside. He stopped short, nearly dropping the Styrofoam cup, when he saw her standing by her bed. Worse, she had pulled off her nasal cannula and was working on her IV. She was so intent on her task that she hadn't heard him.

He set his coffee down on a chair by the door and strode over to her. "What the hell are you doing?"

She whirled around and then swayed. He caught her against him when she would have fallen. She winced when she made contact with his body.

"I have to get out of here," she said desperately.

He held her to his chest, feeling the erratic beat of her heart. It had been so long since he had held her. He picked her up, mindful of her injuries, and placed her back on the bed. She was light in his arms. Too light. She had gotten way too damn thin.

He held up her arm to inspect the IV. Satisfied that it was secure, he looped the plastic tubes over her ears and slipped the cannula back in place. "You aren't going anywhere."

Her lips formed a tight line, but he could see the panic, the fear in her eyes, and it pissed him off. What was she so afraid of? Who had done this to her? To Mom and Pop?

He sat down beside the bed and leveled a hard stare at her. "Now, suppose you tell me where it is you're in such a hurry to go."

"I'm not safe here... You're not safe here."

His brow wrinkled as he looked curiously at her. He hadn't wanted to bombard her with questions so quickly, but if he didn't now, he might not get another chance.

"Where have you been, baby?" he asked softly. "What happened three years ago?"

Chapter Four

Jules stared at Manny, the concern in his eyes nearly her undoing. It was all there in his face. Worry. Anguish. She'd caused it all.

She closed her eyes and turned away. She'd never considered herself a coward. Hell, she'd faced death down more times than she could count, but she couldn't bear to look him in the eye any longer.

"Was it that bad?" he asked, a catch in his voice.

"I don't want to talk about it."

He blew out his breath in frustration, something he'd always done when aggravated.

"I'm sorry, Manny," she offered, trying desperately to keep a tight rein on her emotions. Seeing him, being able to touch him was all she had dreamed of for the last three years. And now that she could, his possible recrimination kept her at a distance. "Please don't hate me. I couldn't bear it if you hated me." Her voice cracked, and she fell silent.

"Jesus, Jules. What on earth are you thinking?" He pulled her almost roughly into his arms. He held her against his chest, her face buried in the warmth of his shirt. She breathed in, content to remain still for just a moment.

Too soon he eased her away and forced her to look at him. "I don't hate you, Jules. Christ, I've dreamed of little else other than seeing you again. Hoping against hope you weren't dead. *Nothing* could make me hate you."

His green eyes probed her intently, his eyebrows furrowed in grave determination. He looked older, and she wondered if she was the cause of the lines around his eyes. Yet another thing to add to her growing pile of guilt. If only she had never gone to France. If only. There were so many if onlys.

Nothing could make me hate you. He had no idea the things she had done. Would he really say that if he knew?

She was tired, so damn tired. She closed her eyes wearily and leaned back against her pillow. When she opened them again, she saw concern flare in Manny's eyes.

"I'm going to have the nurse give you a sleeping pill. You need to rest. You'll be transferring in a few hours."

Alarm shot through her. She couldn't go with Manny. Couldn't place him in danger. Northstar wouldn't hesitate to kill anyone who got in his way. Until she could find a way to be free of the bastard, no one close to her would ever be safe.

Her mind whirling, she nodded slowly. She still had the pill she'd been given earlier. She hadn't wanted anything that would dull her senses. Coupled with the one she would be given now, it might be enough to put Manny to sleep.

When he rose to consult the nurse, she slipped her hand under her pillow and pulled out the pill she had hidden there.

A few seconds later, a cheerful younger woman walked in carrying a tray. "I brought you another cup of coffee," she said to Manny.

"Thanks." He took the cup from her with an expression akin to extreme relief.

She directed her attention to Jules and gave her the same option she had earlier. "Can you swallow another pill or shall I give you an injection?"

"I can swallow it," Jules said in a low voice.

The nurse poured a glass of water, and Manny took it and the pill from her. He walked to the side of the bed and helped Jules sit forward with his free arm. Jules took the pill with the hand she'd palmed the other pill with and quickly shoved both in her mouth. She took a sip of water and made a show of swallowing, but she rolled the pills under her tongue. She'd have to hurry before they dissolved.

"I'll be back to check on you a little later," the nurse said before leaving.

"Thank you," Jules murmured.

As soon as the nurse walked out, Jules glanced over at Manny, who had sat down with his cup of coffee. "Can I have a sip?"

He lifted an eyebrow. "I didn't realize you drank coffee. You always hated it before."

"I don't really, but I remember you always drank it. The smell reminds me of you."

He smiled and handed her the cup. "Careful you don't burn yourself."

As she put the cup to her lips, her stomach lurched at the idea of ingesting the nasty brew, but she tilted it back, shoving the pills from her mouth into the steaming liquid.

She held onto it for a moment, giving the pills time to dissolve before she handed it back to Manny. Hopefully she wouldn't have to wait long. She didn't have much time before he transferred her out.

Knowing she had to be convincing, she settled back with a yawn and closed her eyes. The temptation to give in to sleep was strong. She was tired, more tired than she'd ever been in her life. She focused on the faces of her parents, anything to give her a sense of purpose. Then her thoughts drifted to Manny. She couldn't lose him too. Even if it meant remaining as far away from him as possible.

After what seemed an interminable amount of time, she cracked open one eye and peeked over at Manny. He was yawning broadly and was slouched in his chair. He looked at the coffee in disgust, as if wondering why it wasn't keeping him awake, then impatiently drained the last sip.

A twinge of guilt nipped at her. She was betraying him in the worst way. He would be hurt and not understand why she'd left. But she could take his censure if it meant he would stay alive.

She continued to watch him from the corner of her eye. He shifted restlessly and rubbed his eyes then checked his watch. Once he glanced over at her, and she held her breath, hoping he wouldn't figure out she wasn't asleep. When she was about to scream in frustration, his eyes fluttered closed, and his head sank to his shoulder.

She lay there another twenty minutes, wanting to give him a chance to slip into deep sleep. Then she quickly pulled out the IV, careful to leave it dripping so the alarm didn't go off and alert the nurse.

Now more than ever, she wished Manny had gone out to get her clothing. Being seen running around in a hospital gown was the quickest way to draw unwanted attention.

Noiselessly, she slipped from the bed, her bare feet hitting the cold floor. She closed her eyes for a moment and braced herself against the pain. After several ragged breaths, the discomfort abated, and she straightened cautiously.

There was only one way out. Through the guards posted at her door. She wrinkled her nose in distaste. She needed to conserve as much energy as possible, and right now she felt as weak as a kitten.

With a sigh, she walked over to the door and cracked it open. To her relief, she only saw one man outside her door. Maybe the other was on a coffee break. Which meant she needed to hurry before he returned. She gestured frantically to the guard. "Quick, come here!"

He shot toward the door, and she opened it wider for him. When he was completely within the room, she struck with incredible speed. Planting her elbow sharply in his diaphragm, she left him gasping for breath. Before he could react, she brought her clasped fists down on the back of his neck. He crumpled soundlessly to the floor.

Pain and dizziness assaulted her, but she couldn't give in to them. Not wasting any more time, she stuck her head out the door, looking both ways. To her relief the hall was empty. She slipped out of her room and ran to the stairwell at the end of the hall.

Her breath coming in rapid spurts, she hurried down the stairs to the first level. Her head spun crazily, the pain nearly overwhelming her. She couldn't stop.

If she could find some hospital scrubs, they would make her less conspicuous than the thin gown she wore. On the first level, she peered out of the doorway to the stairwell, trying to decide which way to go. She chose right and followed the signs toward surgery. She held her breath every time she passed another person, but they were all in a hurry, paying no attention to her.

Finally she came to the surgery ward and began trying doors. She found linen closets, personnel offices, but no scrubs. Finally, at the end of the hall she hit pay dirt. Stacks of neatly folded scrubs lay on shelves. She tore off her gown and pulled on pants and a top. She then yanked a cap over her short hair, tucking strands up under the elastic. Lastly, she pulled on shoe covers. They wouldn't offer much in the way of warmth, but they'd at least keep her feet dry for a little while.

Anyone would be hard-pressed to identify her as the ragged girl who had lain in a third-floor bed. She set out for the nearest exit, needing to put as much distance between her and the hospital as possible before her disappearance was discovered.

When she stepped outside, the brisk air washed over her, giving her a much-needed boost. She lengthened her stride and soon disappeared from the parking lot into the wooded area behind the hospital.

She had no money, none of her supplies, and she desperately needed rest. When Manny woke, he'd be pissed. And he'd come looking for her. If he called the cops in, they'd canvass the area and quickly spread out in the directions leading from town. They'd likely assume she'd get the hell out of Dodge.

But they'd be wrong. If she could lie low, they'd eventually fan out beyond her, and she could move in relative obscurity behind their footsteps. Then she could plot her next move.

First she had to find a hiding place, though.

She trudged through the mud from a fresh rain, winding through the trees toward distant lights. Dampness seeped into the thin material over her feet, rendering the covering ineffective. Night was rapidly falling, a fact she was grateful for. She could move easier in the shadows.

Below her, an upscale subdivision spread out over several blocks. Shedding the shoe covers, she squatted down beside a tree and surveyed each residence, looking for one where nobody was at home. It wasn't a lack of lights she looked for. Most people tended to leave lights on even when they weren't at home—an effort to deter burglars. What she looked for was movement. She was patient. Perched close to the ground, she focused on the few houses she couldn't immediately rule out and waited.

Deciding on one at the end of a cul-de-sac, she crept forward, careful to remain in the shadows. When she reached the back edge of the property, she pulled herself up and over the wooden privacy fence and dropped to the ground on the other side. She couldn't go on much farther. She felt lightheaded, woozy, and the pain was becoming harder to ignore.

She surveyed the back of the house, looking for the telltale sticker on a window or door advertising that the house had a security system. Finding none, she chanced moving toward the back door. It was locked, something she had expected. She'd prefer not to break in if she could avoid it. She moved to a set of windows not far from the door and tried each one.

A surge of elation swept over her when one slid quietly upward. Throwing her leg over the sill, she slipped inside, closing the window behind her. She did a quick survey of the house. Typical four-bedroom suburban house. Large kitchen, two family rooms, three bathrooms, dining room and master suite.

During her search of one of the bathrooms, she found several boxes of hair color. So the woman of the house liked to experiment, if the multiple colors were any clue.

Jules chose a box of red and quickly went about wetting her hair in the sink and applying the color. She didn't know how much time she had, and she intended to make the most of it.

When she was finished, she surveyed the end result in the mirror. It wasn't the best dye job in the world, but it achieved the desired effect. She had gone from being a blonde to a redhead. At least temporarily.

Careful to layer the box under the trash already in the garbage can, she exited the bathroom and went in search of a place to rest and lay low. If the people who owned the house had a guest room, chances were when they returned, they wouldn't even know she was there. And if they discovered her, she'd cross that bridge when she got there.

She entered a room less cluttered than the others and assumed this was a spare bedroom. She eyed the bed, a four-poster with a bedspread that swept the floor on all sides. From her vantage point by the door, she couldn't see under the bed. Perfect, as long as there was room for her.

The plush carpet felt good to her bare feet as she padded to the other side of the bed. Kneeling on the floor, she lifted the skirt of the bedspread and peered underneath. Triumph surged through her veins. Her thin frame would fit easily.

She slithered underneath the bed and curled into a comfortable position. Fatigue was overpowering all rational thought. For now she had to rest. She couldn't go on any more. Tomorrow she'd figure out a way to get to Denver and to the duffle bag she had stowed in the locker at the bus depot.

Chapter Five

Manuel stirred and opened his eyes, his mind fuzzy and disjointed. He hadn't meant to fall asleep. Hadn't even realized he was so tired.

As the room came into focus, he saw a man crumpled on the floor in front of him. He came awake instantly and surged to his feet. *Jules.*

He swung around to find the bed empty and swore. Throwing open the door, he stumbled into the hall, looking in both directions. The nurse in the hallway gave him an inquisitive look.

"Where is she?" he demanded. "Did you see her?"

"Who are you talking about?" the nurse asked as she drew closer.

"Jules. She's gone."

The nurse dropped her tray and sprinted toward the nurse's station. After a few seconds the intercom system blared out a message for hospital personnel to be on the lookout for a patient matching Jules's description.

Manuel slipped back inside and took the guard's pulse. It was strong. Manuel strode toward the bed, glancing quickly around for some sign of struggle. The IV line hung limply to the floor, a pool of liquid spreading underneath it.

His gaze lighted on his coffee cup, the one Jules had asked for a drink out of. "Fucking idiot," he swore at himself. Jules had never drunk coffee a day in her life. She'd drugged him.

Worry then anger flashed over him. What the hell was she running from, and why didn't she trust him? He didn't know this Jules at all. She wasn't the same woman he'd loved for so long. For the first time since she'd disappeared, hope died a long death.

He strode from the room, pulled out his cell phone and punched in Tony's number.

"What's up, man?"

"Jules is gone," Manuel bit out.

"What do you mean gone?"

"As in drugged me and disappeared."

"Oh shit. Have any leads on her?"

"I'm searching the hospital now, but I imagine she's got a pretty good head start."

"Manuel," Tony began, then broke off. Silence hung over the phone line.

"Yeah."

"Stop thinking of her as little Jules Trehan. Think of her as an assignment. You need a clear head for this. You can track anyone. You just need objectivity."

"I know." He sighed. This was going to suck. "I need you to notify the local police. Put an APB out on her, but be careful to list her as a missing person, not a possible criminal." An image of the guard in the hospital room flashed across his mind. "On second thought, forget the local police. I don't want her to feel threatened. I'm not sure what she would do. Do we have anyone local?"

"Not sure. I'll have to do some hacking to find out," Tony said with a little too much excitement.

Manuel cursed his own indecision. Calling in other agents, while helpful, would also place Jules at greater risk. Never before had he suffered a lack of trust in his own agency, but it couldn't be construed so much as a lack of trust as it was the knowledge that other agents would be bound to a code he himself wasn't currently following. If Jules was in trouble, she needed help. Someone else would just haul her in for questioning.

"Hold off on the agents, Tony. I need...I need to find her first and figure out what the hell is going on. Have you discovered who was behind the explosion yet?"

"No, sorry. I'm working on it. I've got all my feelers out, and I haven't been able to pick up anyone off our nasty list who's within a hundred miles of where you are."

"Okay, thanks, man."

"No problem. I'll let you know if something turns up. In the meantime, go find your girl."

Manuel hung up and slipped the phone back into his pocket. *Your girl.* Maybe she had never been his. Whatever force had conspired to shove a two-year-old baby girl into his life twenty-three years ago was now tearing her from him. But for twenty years she had been his. His best friend. The one person apart from the Trehans who truly belonged to him.

He had to find out what had happened in those three years she was missing. That was the key to getting her back. And if he could get her back, he would damn sure never let her go again.

For now he was going to take Tony's advice. She was no longer someone who meant the world to him. She was just like any other target he had to hunt down. And he'd never failed yet.

His cell phone rang again, and he looked down at the screen in annoyance. Sanderson.

"Boss man," Manuel acknowledged.

"Manuel, Tony told me what happened."

Manuel waited for Sanderson to continue, hoping he'd make it quick.

"I know how long you've looked for Jules. I know how it must feel to find her after all this time. But you need to be careful. Things aren't looking good so far. She's mixed up in some bad shit."

Manuel's stomach tightened. "What are you saying, Sanderson? Just spit it out, for God's sake."

"I'm saying it doesn't appear she's an innocent victim here. If you find her, I want you to bring her in."

Manuel stood in silence, stunned by Sanderson's order. "Bring her in? What the fuck for?"

There was a long pause. "I've allowed you a lot of latitude in your search for Jules, and now that you've found her, it appears she could be a person of interest to the CIA. I want you to bring her in."

Manuel cursed again and realized his earlier fears were well-founded. Thank God he hadn't had Tony call the local police or other agents.

"And Manuel, that's an order."

Jules opened her eyes, surprised to see light creeping underneath the bed. Damn it. She'd slept the entire night. She carefully lifted the edge of the bedspread and peered out. The door to the bedroom was still closed, and a quick look around the floor told her she was alone.

Cautiously, she edged out from underneath the bed, stretching her aching muscles. Judging by the brightness outside, it was well past eight. She cursed again. How was she ever going to get around without someone seeing her?

She glanced around the room, looking for clothing she could put on. The hospital scrubs, while ideal to get her out of the hospital, were now a flashing beacon.

Were the homeowners home? She hadn't heard any noises in the house. What day was it anyway? She tried to focus, her head still pounding viciously. It was Saturday. She groaned. Everyone in the neighborhood would be home.

The window in this room was large enough for her to go out so she wouldn't have to chance moving through the house. Tiptoeing across the carpeted floor, she was just about to slide open the window when the doorknob rattled.

Jules froze. The door swung open, and she met the startled gaze of a middle-aged woman carrying a laundry basket. The woman let out a shriek then dropped the basket. Could things get any worse?

"What are you doing in my house?" the woman demanded, hands on her hips. Her blonde hair, the product of one of the many bottles Jules had found in the bathroom, was teased and piled high on her head. Her T-shirt was stretched tight across an ample bosom and in big red letters read *Jesus Freak*. Oh yeah, things could definitely get worse.

Jules arched an eyebrow, surprised by the woman's approach. No hysterics. No run to the phone to call 911. No, this woman was pissed and obviously not in the least intimidated by Jules.

"I'm sorry," Jules said softly. "I needed a place to rest." She purposely twisted her hands in front of her, adding to her pathetic air.

"You poor dear," the woman said, surprising Jules by pushing forward into the room. "Are you hiding from a man? Did he do this to you?"

It took Jules a moment to realize the woman was referring to her battered appearance. Was she nuts? She had no idea who this intruder was or if she was armed or dangerous. She *should* be calling 911, not acting like an over-concerned mother hen.

"I had an accident," she said truthfully. "I couldn't stay in the hospital. Someone is looking for me. I just needed a place to rest. And now I have to be going."

"Have you eaten? Because you look too thin," the woman said, ignoring her statements.

Jules loathed her weakness. She should have just taken the woman out, removed any liability to herself. A year ago, she wouldn't have thought twice. She would have just acted to protect herself.

But she hated the person she'd been even more than she hated her current fragility.

"I appreciate your concern, ma'am. But I really should be going. I've imposed on you far too much."

"Polite young thing," the woman clucked. "Too many young people these days are just plain rude. It's nice to see one with manners. Now come downstairs and let me at least fix you a sandwich before you go. Do you have clothes?"

Jules's head was spinning. The woman was an F5 tornado. She reminded her of her own mother. Well, in a perverse sort of way. She didn't have much in common with Frances Trehan, but her protective manner was reminiscent of Jules's beloved mom. Her throat swelled. *Weak.* She was turning into a weak idiot. And it would get her killed.

"If you have a shirt and some jeans, I'd appreciate it," Jules said. "And I'd love a sandwich."

The woman beamed at her. "My name is Doris. Doris Jackson. Come along, dear. I'll have you fixed up and you can be on your way."

"Mrs. Jackson," Jules called out as the woman turned to leave the room.

She paused and looked back at Jules. "Yes, dear?"

"Promise me you'll call the police if you ever find anyone else in your house. You could get hurt."

She chuckled. "Don't worry. If I didn't think I could take you, I would have screamed the house down. But you didn't look like you could hurt a fly in your condition."

Jules nearly laughed. If she only knew. "Appearances can be deceiving, Mrs. Jackson. Don't make the mistake of being nice to an intruder again."

A few minutes later, Jules was attired in a soft long-sleeved sweater and a pair of jeans that almost fit her perfectly. A pair of worn sneakers completed the outfit.

"They were my daughter's," Mrs. Jackson explained. "She's off at college now."

Jules smiled and nodded. She was unused to being around chatty people, and while it comforted her, she wasn't sure how to respond.

In the kitchen, Mrs. Jackson clicked around in her high heels and prepared three sandwiches, tossing them in a bag with numerous other snacks and a few soft drinks. "Here you are, dear. You be careful, okay?"

Jules took the bag and smiled at the older woman. "Thank you. I won't forget your kindness."

"Can I drive you anywhere? Perhaps you shouldn't be walking."

Jules wanted to refuse. She didn't want to place Mrs. Jackson in any danger, but if she drove Jules out of the subdivision, the chances of being seen would be far less. At the same time, if Mrs. Jackson was questioned about her later, this would be a prime opportunity to lay a false trail.

"Could you drive me to the bus station? I would be very grateful."

"Of course. Let me get my keys." She squeezed Jules's hand as she passed, and Jules snatched it away as if she had been bitten.

She was mortified at her reaction, but she wasn't used to being touched. After three years of isolation, she had, in the space of twenty-four hours, been hugged by her mother, held by the man she cared about more than life itself, and comforted by a well-meaning stranger. It was enough to put her in sensory overload.

They drove to the bus station in silence, Jules scanning the surroundings outside her window. When they arrived, Mrs. Jackson dug into her purse and pulled out several twenties. She thrust them at Jules.

"I can't take it." Jules pushed her hand away. "You've been far too kind as it is."

"You remind me of my daughter," Mrs. Jackson said softly. "And I can't bear the thought of you out here all alone. Let me at least buy you a ticket to where you're going."

She blew out her breath then took the money Mrs. Jackson offered. "And you remind me of my mother." She could almost smell the butter and vanilla scent that was so familiar to her. "Thank you." She climbed out of the car and hurried away before Mrs. Jackson could respond.

As soon as the car was out of sight, Jules stepped out of the bus depot and hurried down the street. She fingered the wad of bills Mrs. Jackson had given her. The beginnings of a plan came to her. At least her brain wasn't completely fried.

After getting directions to a local boutique, she headed in that direction. If she was going to pull off her plan, she needed to look hot.

Chapter Six

Manuel stood outside the sixth door he had knocked on and waited impatiently for an answer. He was getting nowhere fast. He'd found the discarded shoe covers in the hills above the subdivision. Wet and muddy, hospital issue. Yeah, Jules had been close, and she might have sought refuge in one of these houses.

The door finally opened and a forty-something lady with frizzy blonde hair stood looking questioningly at him. Emblazoned across her chest were the words *Jesus Freak*.

He flashed a badge, one that identified him as a local policeman, and left it open long enough for her to get a good look. "Good afternoon, ma'am. I wonder if you could help me. I'm looking for someone, and I wonder if you've seen her." He held out a picture of Jules with his other hand.

Fingers with long, well-manicured, fire-engine-red nails plucked the picture out of his hand and held it up. She pursed her lips then held the photo back out to him. "Sorry, haven't seen her."

Manuel frowned slightly and studied her expression. Something odd flickered in her eyes. It looked like anger. And she hadn't asked him any questions as so many of the other neighbors had.

"If you could just take another look," he cajoled. "It's very important that I find her. She's in a lot of danger."

Again, some nameless emotion flickered in her eyes. This time he read uncertainty. Excitement mounted within him.

She leveled a hard stare at him. "I said I haven't seen her. Now if that is all?"

He had to get inside the house. "Thank you for your help, ma'am. Do you mind if I use your bathroom?"

She looked suspiciously at him, and for a moment, he thought she'd refuse. "Can I see your identification again?"

He held the badge with his photo and "name" up to her once more. After a long perusal, she pinched her lips together and opened the door wider. "Down the hall on the right."

He breathed a sigh of relief. If the woman had any sense, she would have slammed the door in his face. How many cops would actually ask to use someone's facilities while in search of a suspect? He smiled reassuringly at her and stepped inside, his gaze absorbing every detail as he slowly walked down the hall. Some of the rooms were open as he passed, and he took quick stock. If only he had time to search the whole house.

He stepped inside the large bathroom and shut the door behind him. After a moment he flushed the toilet then hurriedly opened the cabinets, rifling through the contents. He had no idea what he was looking for, perhaps something to tell him Jules had been there.

He turned on the faucet like he was washing up then transferred his attention to the garbage can. He carefully picked away the top layer. Toilet paper, a few tissues, a wad of hair. Yuck. An empty box of hair dye. No doubt the woman changed her hair color every week. A few cotton balls. Damn. Nothing out of the ordinary.

He stood up and turned the faucet off, disappointment tightening his features. He opened the door to go when his gaze flitted back over the box of hair color. Red.

Frowning, he stared at it for a long moment. The woman was blonde. A fresh blonde judging by the consistency in the color. No roots showing, and no hint of red.

A slow smile spread across his face. "I got you, Jules," he murmured. Why the lady was going to such lengths to protect her he couldn't understand, but then Jules was proving to be more of a challenge than he could have possibly imagined.

Leaving the bathroom, he walked back to the foyer where the woman waited by the door. She frowned at him again. "You aren't going to hurt that young lady you're looking for, are you?"

"No ma'am," he said with utmost sincerity. "I care a great deal about her, and I'm going to find her before some rather unsavory people do."

She studied him for a long moment then laid a hand on his arm. "I probably shouldn't tell you this, but you seem like a sincere young man, and well, I've been told on more than one occasion that I'm a trusting old fool."

"What is it?" he asked. "Did you see her?"

"I took her to the bus station this morning. Gave her some money for a ticket." She sighed heavily then pinned him with a determined glare. "If you hurt that young lady, I'll hunt you down and cut off your balls."

Manuel sobered. "You don't have to worry, ma'am. Jules is very special to me."

The woman's expression softened. "Is that her name? Jules?"

"Yeah. I gave it to her," he said quietly, remembering the day he had named a two-year-old little girl with an unruly mop of curls and innocent blue eyes.

"You find her then and take good care of her."

"I'll do that, ma'am. Thank you for helping her."

"I just wish I could have done more," she said with a frown as Manuel backed out of the doorway. "Poor thing looked like death warmed over."

Manuel's stomach clenched as he waved to the woman and headed for his car. Jules was in no condition to be running all over the country. She needed to be in a hospital bed resting.

He drove immediately to the bus depot and headed inside. Doubt nagged at him as he surveyed the terminal. It was too obvious. And one thing he was fast learning about Jules was that she did nothing that was obvious.

Still, on the off chance that she'd slipped up, he questioned the person at the ticket counter. He struck out there and turned his attention to the passengers waiting for buses. Twenty minutes later, he knew his suspicions had been right.

The woman had driven her here, but had Jules actually left on the bus? More and more he was convinced that Jules wanted it to look like she had.

Manuel walked out of the bus station and continued down the street. He had a lot of ground to cover and not much time to do it in.

Jules breathed a huge sigh of relief as she climbed down from the cab of the eighteen-wheeler and waved goodbye. She teetered unsteadily on the high heels she was wearing and quickly adjusted her sunglasses.

47

"Sure I can't do anything else for you, sweet thing?" the trucker asked with a broad smile.

"You've been more than kind," she said through gritted teeth. She slammed the door and hobbled into the truck stop.

At least four sets of eyes followed her into the bathroom. She couldn't get out of this clothing quick enough. The miniskirt gave new definition to the word *mini*. She stripped it off in disgust and dug out a pair of jeans from her bag. The sneakers Mrs. Jackson had given her were decidedly more comfortable than the three-inch heels she'd donned in Grand Junction. She pulled a T-shirt over her head then put on a zip-up sweat jacket with a hood.

When she was dressed, she began washing the heavy makeup off her face. Then she pulled off the platinum blonde wig she had stolen off a mannequin and brushed her red hair behind her ears.

The reflection in the mirror was of a young college student, not the siren who had flirted with a trucker to get a ride to Denver. Now all she had to do was go to the building where she had rented an apartment and recover the locker key. Not so easy when she was sure the apartment was staked out.

Stuffing the clothes into the garbage can, she eased out of the bathroom and headed back outside. As expected, no one paid her any attention. She was scruffy compared to the blonde bombshell who'd just come in.

Manny. Her insides twisted. Was he looking for her? She knew the answer to that. He was probably frantic with worry. Guilt riddled her gut for what she had done.

You didn't have a choice. He was someone Northstar would use against her to gain her compliance. Just as he had done for the last three years. And if she refused, Manny would die. Just like her parents had.

Still, it didn't make her feel any better about betraying him. She wondered if he used the same cell phone. She had long ago committed the number to memory. No. She couldn't chance it.

What would it hurt? At least he would know she was safe. It wasn't like calling Northstar, where he'd know where she was inside of five seconds. This was Manny. And it was killing her to imagine the agony he must be enduring. He'd already lost the Trehans.

She closed her eyes. She'd call him from the bus station. For now, she had to get going.

She put several blocks between her and the truck stop before stopping at a pay phone to call a cab. After fifteen minutes, the cab pulled up, and she instructed him to drive to the downtown high-rise apartment building she'd briefly stayed in.

Denver. The Mile High City. Even in her circumstances, she'd appreciated the beautiful city when she had first arrived weeks ago. It was a study in contrast. So modern and sleek against the backdrop of the rugged Rocky Mountains.

Something about those mountains called to her. They had told her she could hide in them and never be found. But they had lied.

She blinked when the cab came to a stop. "Can you wait for me? I'll just be a minute."

The cabbie grunted a reply, and she quickly got out. Though it appeared she stared straight ahead, she took in her surroundings, relying on her instincts.

She headed for the concierge's desk. His eyes flickered in recognition when he saw her. She leaned in close. "The envelope. Do you still have it?"

His wary gaze went beyond her as he surveyed the room. Reaching down, he dug a manila envelope out of a drawer and slid it across the counter to her.

She thanked him then took the envelope and hurried out to the waiting cab. "To the bus station on Nineteenth Street," she instructed.

She settled back against the seat and tore open the envelope. To her relief, everything she had put in it was still there. Money, multiple passports and, most importantly, the key. She wouldn't feel totally safe until she had retrieved the contents of her locker.

Several long minutes later, she got out at the bus station and hurried inside after paying the cabbie. She shouldered through the people in the terminal and walked in the direction of the lockers. Two people were there storing away items, and so she waited until they were finished before she scanned the numbers, looking for fifty-four. She inserted the key into the lock and yanked it open. A large black bag hung from a hook. She glanced around again to make sure she wasn't being watched then reached in and grabbed the bag.

She stuffed the envelope inside the bag, not taking the time to survey the contents. It was all there, and with the security cameras present all over the depot, she couldn't afford to raise any suspicion.

Slinging it over her shoulder, she walked in the direction of the pay phones, warring with herself over whether to call Manny or not.

She stood in front of the booth holding the receiver in her hand. A few seconds wouldn't hurt. Just enough time to let him know she was okay. And that she was sorry.

She punched in the numbers to a long-ago memorized calling card and waited with a sick stomach.

He answered on the second ring.

"Manny?"

"Jules. Where are you?" He sounded angry.

"I can't tell you that."

"I see. And what *can* you tell me?"

"That I'm sorry," she said after a long pause. "I know you don't understand, but I just wanted you to know…"

"What do you want me to know?"

"I love you, Manny, and I don't want you to get hurt. And if you're anywhere near me, I can't guarantee that you won't die just like…like Mom and Pop did." She closed her eyes and bit her lip.

"Jules, baby." His voice softened. "There's a lot you don't know about me."

"There's even more you don't know about *me*. And I won't be responsible for your death. You're the only person I have left in this world, and if it means never seeing you again, then I can accept that. At least you'll be alive."

"Just tell me where you are, Jules. I'll come and get you."

"I've got to go, Manny. I love you."

"Damn it, Jules—"

She hung up and leaned her forehead on the receiver.

She shuffled back to the ticket counter and surveyed the schedule. The next bus out was to Kansas City. She'd go there and plot her next move.

After purchasing the ticket, she walked to the correct terminal and checked the clock on the wall. Fifteen minutes until it departed. The bus was just pulling in and letting passengers off. Then she could get on.

She tapped her foot impatiently as the people swarmed off the bus. Again she glanced at the clock, irritated to note the departure was behind schedule. The fifteen minutes had stretched to twenty-five. Finally, the last passengers got off, and she started forward.

"Going somewhere, Jules?"

Chapter Seven

Jules froze then slowly turned around. Her face was ashen, her blue eyes large in her face. "Manny? How did you...?"

"The wonders of modern technology."

"But how?" She looked at him in complete bewilderment. At least she wasn't running. Yet.

"I was already in Denver when you called. I was able to keep you on long enough to pinpoint your location."

"But I used a calling card." She shook her head in disbelief. Not just any calling card, but a code that routed her call through half the freaking world. No way should he have been able to trace her call. "I don't understand. How could you possibly trace my call? Who *are* you?"

Fear crept into her eyes, and his stomach turned over. The last thing he wanted was for her to be afraid of him.

"Do you really want to have this conversation here?" he asked, gesturing at all the people milling about.

Her eyes darted around, still luminous with fear. "You have to get away from me, Manny. If you're seen with me..."

She trailed off, but her meaning was clear.

"Stop trying to protect me, Jules. It's my job to protect you now."

She blew out her breath in frustration. "You don't understand."

"I understand that you are going with me. Now." He enunciated each word and stared intently at her, refusing to back down.

She shrank away as he reached out for her arm.

"Don't make me pick you up and carry you out of here, Jules."

"Don't threaten me." Anger flashed in her eyes. Her hands shook discernibly. She looked close to her breaking point.

Knowing he would win no arguments, he simply plucked her up and cradled her against his chest. She lay there stunned, her mouth open. Then she started struggling.

He tightened his grip on her. "You're making a scene. Do you want everyone to notice you?"

She stilled instantly, but she glared up at him. "Put me down."

"I'll put you down if you agree to come with me."

"Okay, damn it. Just let me go."

He let her slide from his arms, but he kept a tight hold on her hand. "My car is outside. Let's go."

He pulled her along behind him and all but shoved her into the sleek BMW he had driven to Denver. "Put your seatbelt on," he directed as he slid into the driver's seat.

She glared at him again but complied.

"By the way, red isn't your color."

Her mouth tightened, and she stared defiantly out the window. Then she turned back to him, her eyes blazing. "How did you find me? How did you recognize me?"

Manuel keyed the ignition but didn't put the car in gear. He glanced over at Jules. "Do you honestly think a little hair dye is going to make me not see you?" he asked softly. "When your face, your body, everything about you has been imprinted in my soul for the last three years? Did you think I'd forget?"

She stared at him, distress radiating from her like a beacon. She was obviously upset, not that he was here, but that he had found her.

"You can't be near me, Manny. Mom and Pop died because they came to see me. You have to let me go."

There was no way that was going to happen, but he wasn't going to waste precious time arguing with her. "There's a lot you don't know about *me*, Jules. But what is most important right now is that you know *I'm not letting you go again.*"

Her intake of breath was swift. "Manny, I couldn't bear it if I lost you too." Raw agony infiltrated her voice.

"You aren't going to lose me, Jules. Trust me."

She looked startled, as if the idea of trusting anyone was anathema.

He put the car in reverse and backed out of the parking space. Then he roared out of the lot en route to the interstate. He dug out his cell phone and punched in Tony's number.

"Yeah," Tony said in a distracted voice.

"I've got her."

"Hey, that's great. Is she okay?"

Manuel looked over at her. "Yeah, as well as can be expected. You got a safe house worked out yet?"

"Sure do. I'll punch in the coordinates and upload it to your car's navigational system. Just follow the directions, and you'll be there in a few hours."

"What would I do without you, Tony?"

"Die a fiery death, no doubt. I'll check in with you later. I have some information about your girl I think you'll find very interesting."

Manuel sobered. "Tony, I need a favor. One I have no right to ask."

"Shoot."

Manuel sucked in his breath as he contemplated what he was about to do. "Don't let Sanderson know I've found her."

The phone went silent. "Any reason why?" Tony finally asked.

"He wants me to bring her in. I'm not ready to do that yet. There's too much I need to know. Just give me a few days. Run interference for me."

Tony paused again. "Sure man, you got it."

Manuel let his breath out in relief. "Thanks, Tony. I'll keep in touch."

He shoved the phone back into his pocket and turned his attention to the road. What would Tony tell him about Jules? Dread curled in his stomach, spreading up into his chest. Was he prepared to learn what had happened three years ago? Would it change things between him and Jules?

When he glanced over at Jules, he saw that she was staring holes through him.

"Who are you talking about turning me in to? Or not turning me in to? Who the hell are you, Manny?"

"Funny, I was going to ask you the same question." He pinned her with his gaze. "I think we both have a lot of talking to do. When we get to the safe house, I want answers. Until then, you need to get some rest."

He said it in a way that didn't offer her any alternatives. And either she was too tired to argue or she didn't have a response, because she leaned back in the seat and closed her eyes.

Unable to help it, he reached over and curled his fingers around her hand. Warmth spread up his arm when her hand tightened around his.

For the first time, he allowed himself to think everything might be okay. Now if only he could convince her of that.

Jules stared out her window, the miles passing in a blur. She and Manny hadn't exchanged words since they'd left Denver, but she knew he watched her. She could feel his gaze on her, but she refused to meet his stare.

They were heading south toward New Mexico, and with each mile her fear grew. Fear that she wouldn't be able to protect Manny from Northstar. From what she'd become.

She sank lower in the seat, gingerly drawing her knees up to her chest. Her fingers stroked the duffle bag at her side, drawing assurance from the outline of the gun there. At least she'd have some way of defending them when—not if—they were tracked.

A sharp pain twisted through her chest and robbed her of breath. She sucked in air, determined not to panic as the scenery blurred before her. Damn, her ribs were on fire. She reclined the seat in an attempt to alleviate the growing pressure in her midsection.

The pain eased as she stretched out, and her breathing evened. She pressed her hands to her temples and squeezed her eyes shut. Her pulsed thudded incessantly against her fingertips.

"Speak to me, Jules. What's wrong? Do I need to get you back to the hospital?" Manny's concerned voice seared through her haze of pain.

"No," she said faintly. "I'm all right. Really."

"Where are you, baby? Because you're miles away from here right now."

She cringed, not wanting to voice what she had been thinking. It sounded pathetic and defeatist. But she blurted it out anyway. "I was thinking it should have been me who died. Not Mom and Pop."

To her surprise, he slammed on the brakes and pulled over to the shoulder. He turned on her, his eyes blazing in the faint light offered by the headlights. "Don't say that. Don't *ever* say that. I thought I lost you, Jules. For three long years I lived with the awful reality you might not be coming home. And then I found you. Don't you dare wish you had died, because I've spent the last three years praying you were alive."

Before she could respond, he put his hand around the back of her neck and pulled her to meet his kiss. Her mouth opened in surprise, and his tongue darted forward, gently probing her lips.

It was everything she had ever dreamed it would be. For a moment, she was in high school again, dressing for the prom, depressed because the one guy she wanted to take was eight years older and already out of college. She had closed her eyes and imagined it was Manny kissing her when her date had delivered her to the door with the prerequisite peck on the lips.

He was exquisitely gentle, his lips moving reverently over hers. His fingers worked slowly into her hair, kneading and stroking as he deepened his kiss.

Then, as suddenly as it had begun, it ended. He pulled away from her and ran a hand through his hair in agitation. "Christ, I'm sorry, Jules. You don't need that right now."

She stared at him in shock. With a trembling hand, she raised her fingers and touched her swollen mouth.

"Don't look at me like that." He captured her hand and brought it to his lips. "I'm sorry, baby."

He allowed her hand to slide from his, and she pulled hers away, cradling it with her other hand. What was she supposed to say? She was so damn confused she doubted she could recall her own name at the moment. For that matter, she really had no idea what her real name was. A hysterical bubble of laughter rose quickly in her throat, and she fought to choke it back.

Manny swore softly then pulled back onto the highway. "Get some sleep, Jules. If you don't, I swear, I'll call Tony and have you transferred to the hospital like we'd planned. It's what I should've done in the first place."

"Who the hell is Tony anyway?" she grumbled as she lay back against the leather seat. She shivered, and Manny reached over to turn up the heat.

"Tony is my partner."

"Partner in what? Somehow I doubt you're still in the computer software business." He looked far too dangerous to be a computer nerd. She had never been able to reconcile his image with his profession.

"Rest," he said in a warning tone. "We'll talk when we get there."

"Wherever there is."

He smiled.

"What's so funny?"

"You are. You're sounding more and more like the Jules I know all the time."

She sobered instantly, the throbbing in her head resuming with a vengeance. "I'm not her. Maybe I never was."

Manny gripped the steering wheel tighter. "Rest."

Not arguing, she turned to the window. She could never go back to that carefree, naive girl she had once been. She'd seen and done far too much. She was glad Mom and Pop had never gotten to see the person she'd become. Their disappointment would have been more than she could bear.

She raised trembling fingers to her lips, lips still swollen from Manny's kiss. What exactly were his feelings for her? She'd never imagined that he returned her sentiment, that he might want her just as badly as she'd wanted him, but in the face of the way he'd kissed her, she could hardly ignore the possibility. Had she been blind to the signs?

She thought back, trying to analyze Manny's behavior toward her. As a teenager, she'd idolized him, fantasized about being Mrs. Manuel Ramirez, but she'd been careful to keep her girlish imaginings to herself. She would have died if he'd found out the extent of her infatuation.

Three years ago, she would have done anything for Manny to kiss her like he just had, but now it only complicated matters. No matter how much she wanted him to be more than a big-brother protective figure, it wasn't possible. And if he knew the truth about her, he wouldn't want her anyway.

"It's snowing." He turned to her when she looked over. "You used to love the snow."

"Yeah," she said faintly. But she didn't now. It was too easy to be tracked in the snow. She remained silent, not voicing that tidbit of information. Instead she watched the flurry of snowflakes through the windshield wipers.

The heat pouring from the vents and the steady hum of the wipers lulled her into a state of relaxation. Soon her eyes grew as heavy as her heart, and she allowed them to close. Her final thought was that she hoped it wasn't snowing wherever they ended up.

Chapter Eight

Manuel pulled to a stop outside a large log cabin and shut off the engine. He glanced over at Jules who was still sleeping soundly. He hated to disturb her, but he wasn't going to leave her in the car while he went in to check out the cabin. She'd probably bolt. He had seen the resolve in her eyes. She may have conceded defeat for the moment, but he had no illusions that she was suddenly going to become complacent.

He got out, walked around to her side and quietly opened the door. He unbuckled her seatbelt and slipped his arms under her slight form. She came awake instantly.

"Jules, it's okay. It's me."

She reached down for her duffle bag and held it close to her. "I can walk."

He ignored her and scooped her up into his arms. As he headed for the front porch, he examined the area around them. The scent of pine was strong, and in the distance he could hear rushing water. The cabin was up on a slight hill that gave the surrounding area a good view from the inside. On two sides the forest was dense. From the sound, it seemed a river provided a natural barrier between the back of the cabin and the outlying woods. The only opening was the narrow drive leading to the front of the cabin.

Not willing to take any chances, he eased Jules from his arms and put a finger to his lips. "Stay behind me." He drew his gun and cracked open the door. Jules stared at him in surprise but showed no discomfort over the appearance of the weapon.

After a quick run-through of the house, he was satisfied that it was safe to remain. He motioned for Jules to sit on the couch, and he flipped on the lights in the large living room.

She settled on the couch, clutching her duffle bag tight against her chest. He was certain she hadn't had it at the hospital, but where she picked it up he couldn't be sure. Despite his curiosity, he held his tongue, wanting her to calm down before they had their talk.

"Want something to eat?" he asked, turning toward the kitchen.

She stood, and he leveled a hard stare at her. "Sit down, Jules. I'll get us something."

Slowly, she complied. "Okay."

He could see her from the open kitchen, and he was careful to keep a close eye on her as he rummaged through the cabinets. Tony had proved thorough as usual. They could easily survive weeks here if they had to.

"Want some pancakes?" he called.

A ghost of a smile formed around her lips. "That would be great. You always did make the best pancakes."

"They were your favorite."

"I haven't eaten them since the morning I left for France." Her voice cracked, and she looked away.

A rock settled in his stomach. She had been so excited that morning. The Trehans had given her a trip to France to celebrate her graduation from college, and she was bursting at the seams to go. He'd come home to see her off. They had gotten up early so he could cook her favorite breakfast, then he'd driven her to the airport. It was the last time he'd seen her.

The Jules who had left, the ready-to-take-on-the-world girl who wanted to do and see it all, was a far cry from the wounded woman he now faced.

He mixed the batter, adding the ingredients mechanically. At his side, his cell phone vibrated. Wiping his hands, he stole a quick glance at Jules before backing toward the pantry where he would be out of her sight. He snapped up the phone. "Make it quick," he said in a low voice.

"You get to the cabin yet?"

"Yeah, we're here."

"You want what info I have now, or you want to call me back later?"

Manuel expelled a long rush of air. "Let me call you back. I want to hear what she has to say first."

"Okay, give me a holler when you're ready."

"Is it bad?" Manuel asked, suddenly aware that he was holding his breath.

Silence settled over the line. "It ain't exactly good," Tony finally said. "By the way. A heads-up. Sanderson is going to give you a call in a few. He wants to know what the hell is going on. I've played dumb, but I know he's not buying it."

Manuel quietly ended the call and stuck the phone back in his pocket. Why it was so important that he hear it from Jules he wasn't sure. But it had to come from her. He wanted to be looking her in the face when he found out what the hell had happened three years ago. And maybe he wanted to see how honest she would be with him.

On cue, the phone rang again. Manuel saw it was Sanderson and answered.

His boss cut straight to the point. "Manuel, what do you have to report?"

"Nothing yet, sir. I'm still in Denver."

"Do you need more agents on this?" Sanderson asked.

Panic crept up Manuel's spine. "No, sir. I want to do this. I need to. I'll find her."

"All right. Keep me posted. You've got three days, Manuel. Then I call in backup."

The phone went dead, and Manuel cursed vividly under his breath. Three days. It wasn't much time to cover three years. He shoved his phone in his pocket and went in search of Jules.

"Soup's on," he called, rounding the corner into the living room. He looked at the empty sofa. *Fuck!* He glanced around the room, breathing a sigh of relief when he saw her standing by the fireplace.

"Jules?" He crossed the floor and put a hand on her shoulder. She whirled around, her eyes flaring for a moment.

"Didn't mean to startle you. Your pancakes are ready."

She flashed a smile that didn't reach any higher than the corners of her mouth. "Can't wait."

She followed him back and sat down at the table. He put a plate heaped high with pancakes in front of her then took a seat across from her.

He watched as she picked at the food, nibbling a few bites. She looked away most of the time, never at him, never meeting his gaze. Perhaps she knew the time had come.

Still, he waited. He wanted her to eat and relax her guard before they bared their souls. And truth be known, he wasn't sure he was ready to hear what had happened to her. How cowardly of him to be so afraid to know what she had been forced to endure.

If she had been forced.

Her last words to him echoed in his mind, the phone call, the last time he'd spoken to her. Her fear, her terror. It ate at him. Had eaten at him for the last three years. He'd imagined the most awful scenarios, and he prayed that none of them were true.

When she finally shoved the plate away, she looked up at him, and he locked gazes with her. "You know it's time for us to talk."

She closed her eyes and nodded.

He reached over and took her hand. "Don't be frightened, Jules. You don't ever have to be afraid again."

Still holding her hand, he helped her up and led her into the living room. "Sit down. I'll build us a fire."

He quickly stacked wood from the box over a few pieces of kindling then struck a match. In a few seconds, a steady flame licked up over the logs.

Returning to Jules, he settled beside her, his gaze sweeping over her face. She was so fragile-looking he feared touching her. She looked poised to break into a million tiny pieces, and he wondered not for the first time how hard he should press.

He pushed a strand of hair over her ear and let his palm rest against her cheek. "Talk to me, baby."

Her eyes were enormous in her face. Fear, fatigue, apprehension. They all crowded to the front.

Wanting to put her at ease, he pulled her against him, feeling her heart beat frantically against his chest. He stroked her hair then moved his hand up and down her back in a soothing motion.

Her arms crept around him, and his chest tightened uncomfortably. How long he had waited for this moment. For her to be in his arms where she belonged.

Jules tentatively burrowed into his embrace, seeking comfort she'd long been denied. His broad chest cradled her cheek, and she nuzzled deeper into his muscled hardness. She didn't want to talk. Didn't want to unleash her tightly held demons.

She'd held them close for so long, they clawed at her, seeking release. If she hated herself so much, how could everyone else not do the same?

His warm hand cupped her chin and slowly forced her to look up at him. "I can't help myself," he murmured as he lowered his lips to hers.

But the past was burning too brightly in her mind. All she saw were the shadows closing in around her. Frightening images. Suffocating memories.

Her breathing lurched and sped up. Panic. Groping hands. Self-loathing.

Manny jerked away from her, fire in his eyes. He was angry. She'd never seen him angrier. His entire body bristled, power shrouding him. He looked every inch the predator. Gone was her childhood protector, the object of her teenage crush. In his place was a dangerous man. One who looked as though he could take apart someone with his bare hands.

She shivered involuntarily, and his expression grew even blacker.

"Who hurt you, Jules?" he demanded, his voice dangerously low.

It took her a moment for her to realize that he wasn't angry with *her*. He had picked up on her utter terror, and now he was a seething mass of muscle. She opened her mouth to speak, to reassure him in some way, but no words came out.

Her throat was fast closing in, and once again, harsh despair swelled inside her. Though she hated the person she'd become, she recognized that at least *that* person was strong.

He reached hesitantly for her, and she turned away, curling herself into an impenetrable ball. It was all crashing down. Her carefully constructed balance was rapidly deteriorating.

"Manny, I can't breathe," she gasped.

Manuel grabbed her shoulders and turned her back to him. "Look at me, Jules," he ordered. He forced himself to be calm, though he boiled just beneath the surface.

Her eyes flitted up to him, dull, lifeless. He swore long and hard under his breath. This was his fault. He pushed her too hard, too fast. And he couldn't keep his damn hands to himself. Finally being able to hold her, touch her, had overwhelmed him. He needed to be close to her. Reassure himself that she was really here.

"You're safe. Nothing can hurt you anymore. Do you understand me? I won't let anyone hurt you again. Ever."

Regret flickered in eyes that had shone lifeless just seconds before. "It's out of your hands, Manny."

The sound of glass shattering startled them both. Instinctively, Manuel shoved Jules to the floor, shielding her with his body.

Gunshots sounded, the rat-a-tat peppering of bullets spraying through the windows and into the walls on the other side of the cabin.

"Let me up, damn it!"

"Stay down," he barked, reaching for his gun.

She shoved hard at him and reached for her duffle bag, her fingers straining to capture the handles.

"For Christ's sake, Jules. This isn't the time!"

He returned fire, spacing his shots a few inches apart in the direction of the gunshots.

Jules kicked him in the gut, and one of his shots went wild. "What the hell are you doing?"

She managed to snag her bag and tear it open, the contents spilling onto the floor. She grabbed a mean-looking Russian assault rifle in one hand and a Glock in the other.

"Cover me."

"What the... Get back here!"

She rolled across the floor, laying down a spray of fire.

"Son of a bitch." He turned and began firing as well.

The front door burst open, and before he could react, Jules put a bullet straight through the intruder's forehead. She had impressive aim.

She shoved the body over and removed the machine gun from the dead man's grasp. She sent it sliding over the wood floor in Manuel's direction, and he scooped it up, shoving his piece back in his waistband.

Suddenly, she raised her pistol and aimed it straight at his head. He jerked when she fired then heard a thud behind him. He glanced over his shoulder to see another body sprawled on the floor. "Thanks," he muttered.

He caught movement outside one of the shattered windows and immediately fired off a round. A shadowy figure fell. Three down now. How many more were there?

As if reading his mind, Jules called out from her perch by the door. "They usually travel in teams of six."

"And how would you know that?"

"Trust me."

Trust her. How the hell was he supposed to trust her when he didn't have a friggin' clue what her involvement was? All he knew was that since her reappearance, the people he considered his second parents had been blown to hell, he'd been drugged, and now he was being shot at. Not exactly the cornerstones of trust.

And then there was the fact that one minute she was an injured fawn and the next she was an avenging angel, hauling a freaking arsenal out of her gym bag.

He'd had enough of this shit. The gloves were off. If they made it out of this alive, she was going to do some serious explaining. And this time, his damn hormones weren't going to get in the way.

"Follow me," he ordered, gesturing at Jules. His tone brooked no argument, but he wasn't entirely sure she would listen.

To his surprise, she scooted forward, her chest to the floor. "You have a plan, I take it?"

"Yeah. It's called *we're getting the hell out of here.*"

She made a rude noise. "No need to get snippy."

"Save the lip, Jules. You've got a hell of a lot of explaining to do if we make it out of here alive."

"*If* we make it out alive."

He glared at her then crawled toward the back door. He didn't harbor any hope that no one was staking out the exit, but he knew if they could get to the river they might have a chance. Might.

"When I start firing, I want you to dive out the door and keep on going," he directed. "Get to the river. If I don't show up in two minutes, get to the other side and use this." He shoved his phone at her. "Just punch one. Tony will answer."

She stared at him, her eyes determined. "You'll show up or I'll come back and haul your ass out of here."

He kicked the back door open and began laying down a barrage of bullets.

Jules dove onto the porch and rolled off into the snow. Hell. There was already an inch on the ground.

A bullet struck the soft powder beside her head, kicking up icy pellets. She shot in the direction she thought the bullet had come from and scrambled farther into the trees and toward the river.

Behind her, the gunfight continued, the short staccato of the machine gun followed by the longer barking of a high-powered rifle. Then the sound of Manny's pistol. Shit. He'd run out of ammo in the Uzi.

She wasn't about to leave him to the three remaining hit men. Jamming another magazine into her assault rifle, she scrambled back up the hill.

Manny was just inside the door, shooting into the woods to her left. She surveyed the terrain behind him, alarmed to see movement close to the porch. Too close. She raised her gun and squeezed off a round.

Manny jerked around then pinpointed her position with a menacing stare. "Damn it, Jules. Do you ever listen to anyone? Get the hell out of here."

She ignored him, seeking out the remaining two. They were out there. She could feel them. The front was unguarded now that she and Manny had moved to the back. One could be inside even now.

"Get down!" she cried, thankful that Manny immediately dropped to the floor. Unable to get her rifle up in time, she reached for her Glock with her left hand, yanked it up and fired at the man behind Manny.

He fell forward, and Manny recovered his weapon.

"Okay, so I'm glad you didn't go," he grumbled.

He dove from the house, rolling in the snow toward her. To their left, the last assailant peppered the snow in front of Manny. Before she could shoot, Manny rose up on his elbows and shot one time. The fire halted immediately. Eerie silence filtered through the trees.

"Come on," he said, picking himself up. He pulled her back inside, through the living room and toward the front door.

"Wait." She pulled away from him and dropped to the floor. She hastily collected the items from her bag and shoved them back inside. She needed everything.

As she rose, Manny's hand closed around her elbow like a vise grip. "We're getting out of here."

He ushered her outside and all but shoved her into the car. Before starting the engine, he punched a series of buttons on a small device secured to the dash.

"What are you doing?" she asked.

"Making sure it isn't wired with explosives."

"And you can tell that how?" she asked in disbelief.

"I'd love to stop and explain, but I'm more concerned about getting the hell out of here."

She shrugged as he started the engine and threw it into reverse. They tore down the road as fast as the conditions allowed.

"Who are you?" she demanded. "FBI?"

"Not exactly," he said, never taking his eyes off the road.

"What does *not exactly* mean?"

"It means I'm not FBI," he ground out. "Look, can we save the question-and-answer period for later? Maybe when I'm not trying to save our asses?"

She slid down into her seat and stared out the window. Now that the adrenaline rush was gone, her body let her know just how much it didn't appreciate her throwing herself around the cabin. She closed her eyes wearily and pondered the mystery of just who Manny was. Whoever he worked for, he had connections and he knew how to defend himself. Computer software analyst he was not.

If he was FBI or anything similar, she couldn't afford for him to know who she was. Not that it would be safe for him to know under any circumstances. But for the first time, she allowed herself to dwell on what his profession meant for her.

She'd never imagined that he would be in law enforcement, though he certainly looked the part. Menacing. It was the only word to describe him when he was pissed off. He'd be a serious deterrent to anyone wanting to cross the line.

How could she possibly tell him, the enforcer, that she had broken every law he had sworn to uphold?

Chapter Nine

The miles spread out before them as they headed across the barren landscape of West Texas. The first faint shadows of dawn had begun to creep across the eastern horizon, painting the sky lavender.

Silence was thick between them, and Manny still gripped the steering wheel as tightly as he had when they had fled the cabin. He hadn't once looked at her, his eyes fixed on the road ahead of him. He was angry. At her? She wasn't sure, but he was no longer treating her with kid gloves. She greeted that fact with relief.

Hatred, anger she could take. She wasn't used to softness. Gentleness. Caring. She had no idea how to respond to kindness. Maybe now she could stop being a watering pot every time he looked at her.

She sighed and closed her eyes. She had to get away from Manny before he died because of her. The men who had tried to kill them were from the NFR. Under Northstar's direction, she was sure. No matter how much Manny thought he could protect her, he had no idea what he was up against.

In her duffle bag were passports, money, weapons. Everything she needed to get out of the country and draw attention away from Manny. Normally she would be patient, but she didn't have time to wait until an opportunity presented itself. She would have to make her own.

"Whatever it is you're thinking, I can assure you I won't like it."

She turned to look at him as his voice filled the car. "How do you know what I'm thinking?"

"It's not that hard to figure out," he said with a sideways glance at her. "You aren't going anywhere without me, especially not with a bunch of machine gun-wielding maniacs on the loose."

He relaxed his grip on the steering wheel and let out his breath. "Know who those jokers were?"

"I have an idea."

"Care to enlighten me?"

She looked down at her hands. "They're from an organization called the New French Revolution."

"Christ. Nothing like having a bunch of terrorists wanting to kill you."

"You know who they are?" she asked with a frown in his direction. "The NFR is a pretty low-key organization. They never publicly take credit for their hits like so many of the Middle Eastern terrorist cells."

"I think the more important question is why *you* know who they are and why they want to kill you."

"It's complicated." More complicated than he could possibly know. She wasn't even sure she understood her role. Drifting between two worlds, neither good.

"So tell me, Jules, when is a good time? Maybe after I've taken a bullet in the ass?"

"You're angry."

"No, I'm *pissed*," he corrected. "I tend to get that way when I've been shot at."

She arched an eyebrow. "Are you shot at often?"

"Don't change the subject. Why is the NFR after you?"

"They're pissed off at me."

"So am I, but I'm not trying to kill you."

"But they're *really* pissed."

"And why are they pissed, Jules? Terrorist groups don't usually single out an individual. They're much more interested in large masses of people."

"They aren't technically terrorists," she muttered.

He nearly veered off the road. Slowing drastically, he turned to her, his mouth agape. "Jules, why the hell are you *defending* a terrorist organization?"

"I'm not defending them," she protested. And she wasn't. Shit. She should have just kept her mouth shut and let him think what he wanted. "A terrorist and a revolutionary aren't the same thing. A terrorist is, well, a terrorist. They operate on fear. No real or realistic agenda. A revolutionary acts to effect change. They have realistic goals."

"I don't believe I'm hearing this," he said in a strained voice. "Call them what you want. They're goddamn criminals, and they've killed a lot of Americans."

"So has the American government," she said bitterly.

He shook his head, his face reddening. So he was obviously a patriot. She had been one too, in the beginning. Now she just wanted to move to some remote jungle. Away from patriotic duty and the bullshit that was honor.

Another long moment of silence settled over them. She twisted her hands in front of her and took a deep breath. "Manny?"

"Yeah?"

"What happened to Mom and Pop?" Her voice wavered more than she wanted it to, but her parents had died and there hadn't even been so much as a memorial service. Were they lying in a morgue somewhere? Alone and without family to take them home?

"They were cremated," he said quietly. "It was their wish. When all of this is over with, I thought we'd go home and have a memorial service for them."

This. He said it with such distaste. She knew *this* was all her doing. Not only had she killed her parents, but she had prevented them from having a proper burial.

She buried her face in her hands, utter grief overcoming her. She couldn't grieve for her *real* parents. They were killers, like her. But Mom and Pop? Their only sin was taking in a homeless little girl and loving her unconditionally.

"Jules," Manny said, his voice full of regret. He squeezed her shoulder then slid his hand down to grasp hers.

"I loved them, Manny. I know you don't think so, but it was for them that I stayed away. And it was all for nothing." Bitterness spilled from her lips. So much hatred. It was like poison. Felt like venom.

He slowed then pulled over into the parking lot of a truck stop. After turning off the ignition, he shifted in his seat and turned to look at her. "Perhaps you tell me just why it is you did stay away. I never considered even for a moment that you were doing so of your own free will. Are you telling me it was a conscious decision?"

She squeezed her eyes shut. "It isn't that simple."

"Yes, Jules, it is. Either you were prevented from returning home or you chose not to come home. Which is it?"

"You see things as black or white, Manny. Things rarely are, you know."

"No, I don't know. Why don't you explain it to me over a cup of coffee. God knows I could use one," he said wearily.

She wrinkled her nose. "Make mine juice, and I'll take you up on it."

He didn't smile at her. She sighed and got out of the car, stretching cautiously. She winced when pain washed over her. Her ribs were nowhere close to being healed, and she didn't have time to make sure they mended properly.

"Are you okay?" Manny asked beside her, concern reflected in his voice.

She wanted to weep. Despite his anger, he was still worried about her. *Goddamn, Jules. Quit with the crying already.* She slammed her door in disgust and followed Manny into the small diner.

They slid into a booth by a window. Both looked cautiously around as they surveyed the menu. Oh yeah, he was some kind of law enforcement. He had the instincts. And, she admitted to herself, he was damn good. Whatever he was.

A waitress shuffled over to take their order and stood smacking on her gum while she waited for Manny to speak. It was obvious that she was checking him out. Her gaze wandered up and down his body appreciatively, and she stood a little closer than was necessary.

Jules frowned and followed the waitress's avid stare. It had been a long time since she'd looked at a man with anything other than self-preservation in mind. And she had to admit, Manny looked even better now than he had three years ago. Thickly muscled arms and a broad chest. Perfect for melting into and feeling safe.

She coughed to cover the hysterical laughter that threatened to bubble out. When was the last time she felt safe?

Manny's green eyes burned into her. "Is something wrong, Jules?"

She coughed again. "Uh no, just a bit of pain." It wasn't a complete lie. Her chest and lungs felt like shit.

He rattled off his order to the waitress then looked questioningly at Jules. "Want anything else besides juice?"

She shook her head. Her stomach was in enough turmoil without loading it down with food.

When the waitress had left, he leaned over and stared straight at her. "Now, I want to know what happened three years ago. Why didn't you come home? All I got was a phone call from you saying you couldn't ever come home, and you sounded scared to death. Damn it, Jules. Do you have any idea what that was like? There was nothing. Nothing else until a few days ago."

She bowed her head, unable to meet his gaze. "I'm sorry."

"I'm beginning to think I don't know you at all."

"It's not what you think." She raised her head back up. "It's not like I arbitrarily decided not to come home. I would never have done that to Mom and Pop. Or you."

"Then what happened? Did someone hurt you?" The dangerous glint was back in his eyes.

She rubbed her hands back and forth over her arms. "I can't tell you everything—"

"Can't or won't?"

"Okay, won't," she said, her chin snapping up further. "I had no choice but to stay away from you all. I was told that if I didn't do exactly as instructed, they would kill Mom and Pop.

You. And in the end, it didn't even matter. Mom and Pop died anyway."

Manuel stared wordlessly at her, trying to process the information she had given him. "Who is *they*, Jules?" A sudden thought came to him. "Oh God. It was the NFR, wasn't it? They recruited you."

Her silence gave him his answer. "Jesus Christ. You mean to tell me you've been a member of the NFR for the last three years? Is that why you defended them?"

"I wasn't defending them. I merely suggested there were worse groups."

"You didn't answer the question," he growled. "Quit jerking me around and talk to me."

"Yes, Manny. Happy now? I was a card-carrying member of the NFR. I ate, drank and slept all things NFR. All because the one thing that mattered to me was in danger. I became someone I *despised*, because at least it meant my family was alive."

Grief, rage, sadness. They all swam crazily in her eyes. He felt the same things deep in his soul. Was she telling the truth? She had to be. After all, mere days ago, Mom and Pop had died because they had gone to see her.

His cell phone vibrated, and he yanked it up in irritation. "What?" he barked out, never letting his gaze fall from Jules.

"Bad time?" Tony asked.

"You could say that."

"I wanted to make sure you two were okay. Everyone make it out all right?"

"The information you had for me earlier," Manuel bit out, ignoring Tony's question. "Give it to me now."

A long pause. "Uh, okay. Give me a second to get the file."

Manuel waited, his eyes boring into Jules's tormented ones.

Tony's voice came back over the line. "You ready?"

"Yeah."

"It would appear your girl is a highly trained assassin. A damn good one, if my information is correct. Not your average run-of-the-mill terrorist. She's been pretty selective in her hits. If I'm right, she's a member of a splinter cell of the NFR. Not their front line, but a small select group used to focus on individuals detrimental to their cause."

Nausea boiled in Manuel's stomach. He clenched the phone in his hand, wanting desperately to send it through the window. He wanted to break something, anything. He wanted to put his first through the wall.

"You okay?" Tony asked. "I know how much she meant to you."

"Means, Tony. She still means everything to me." He hung up the phone, letting it fall onto the table.

"Your buddy confirm my story?" she asked bitterly.

He shook his head. "I don't understand. I don't even know what to say right now."

"You don't have to say anything," she said, though he could hear the anguish in her voice. "Now maybe you can see why you have to stay away from me. You can't be near me. Ever."

"Bullshit."

She raised her eyebrows.

"You left for a reason, Jules. Why did you come back, and why are they chasing you?"

"They don't take kindly to people leaving the fold."

"Why would you chance leaving now, after three years, if the only reason you stayed was because they threatened Mom and Pop?" There was something about her story that just didn't ring true. That she would lie to him thrust a knife straight into his chest.

"Because I was foolish," she said in disgust. "I thought I was smarter. Thought I could just disappear and no one would care or try to find me. As long as I stayed away from my family, they wouldn't know where I was. I was wrong. I should have just fucked up an assignment and died."

He looked at her in shock. She wasn't being melodramatic. She was dead serious. Had she contemplated death before?

"How did you find me, Manny? Did they contact you?"

"I never stopped looking for you. I've used department resources, manpower, all the technology I have at my disposal, and until a week ago, nothing."

She leaned forward. "Who do you work for? You said not FBI. What then?"

He debated whether to tell her the truth. But he wouldn't lie to her, not like she had to him. "I work for the CIA."

He was unprepared for the revulsion that spread across her face. Had her years with the NFR influenced her so greatly? The NFR was one of five main groups the CIA had spent years trying to infiltrate. The only group they had been unsuccessful with so far.

"The CIA? How long? Were you already working for them before I left for France?"

He nodded. "I joined right after I graduated from college."

She laughed harshly. "So the computer business was all a front?"

He nodded again.

"I was going to ask you for a job when I got back from France."

"And I was going to ask you to marry me." It slipped out before he could recall the words. But it hardly mattered. It was a lifetime ago.

She jerked back as if she had been slapped. "W-what?"

His phone rang again, and this time he really did give serious thought to throwing it through the window.

"This better be good," he snapped.

"You need to get moving," Tony said.

Manuel was immediately on alert, motioning Jules to get up and follow him. He reached into his pocket, pulled out a few bills and threw them on the table. "What's going on?" he asked as he guided Jules outside to the car.

"Satellite picked up a transmission a few minutes ago. Your girl was a topic of conversation. They seem pretty pissed at her. They also know you're headed for Dallas. My suggestion is to turn south to Houston and hop a plane to D.C., pronto. And Manuel, Sanderson is all over me. He knows what I know so far. You need to be careful. If you need to call me, use our backup method, you got me?"

Yeah, Manuel knew what he was talking about. It was a pain in the ass to route the calls through the dozen channels he'd have to go through, but he didn't want the boss man to be breathing down his or Tony's necks.

Manuel slammed Jules's door behind her. "I want a full report later. Dig up what you can about the NFR. Particularly their recruiting tactics. I'll call you as soon as I can."

Chapter Ten

Jules pretended to sleep on the drive to Houston. She could feel Manny watching her. Wanting to question her further. But she had no desire to talk about the years she had spent with the NFR. Not now. Not ever. She'd just as soon forget the whole thing.

She nearly laughed. Kind of hard to forget when they were breathing down her neck. What a fool she'd been to think she could escape so easily.

And now to discover he worked for the agency that held her life, and now his, in its hands. For a brief moment, she entertained the idea that maybe he wasn't as uninformed as he pretended to be, but no, she couldn't believe that of him. In a world where she could believe nothing and trust no one, she clung to the idea that this man was honorable despite the monsters he worked for.

She couldn't tell him the truth. He wouldn't likely believe her anyway. And the truth would get him killed just as quickly as being with her would.

"You can open your eyes, Jules. I know you're awake," Manny said dryly. "We're almost to the hotel."

"I need to stop at a pharmacy or grocery store," she said.

He frowned. "I'd rather you not be exposed unless absolutely necessary."

"I need to dye my hair back. Red's a little noticeable."

He looked like he wanted to question the reason for ever dying it red, but she fixed him with a silencing glare. His lips tightened and he exited the freeway and then pulled into the parking lot of a grocery store.

"Let's make it quick," he said in a low voice.

A few minutes later, they returned to the car, everything Jules needed in a small bag.

They drove up a few exits before Manny pulled off again and into the parking lot of a small airport hotel.

He drove under the awning of the front entrance then turned to look at her. "Can I trust you to stay here while I check us in or do I need to haul you inside with me?"

"I'm not going anywhere."

He stared at her for a long moment then opened his door. He pulled the keys from the ignition and stuffed them into his pocket before stepping out.

She sat and waited, taking in the immediate surroundings. Her eyes soaked in every detail, the proximity to the interstate, the number of cars in the lot. Anything to let her know what she was up against.

A few minutes later, Manny slid back into the car and started the engine. He drove a few feet forward and pulled into a nearby parking space. "Let's go," he said.

She collected her bag and got out, stretching her aching body. She followed behind Manny as they entered the hotel from a side entrance.

The room was nothing fancy, the bedspreads and draperies faded and thin. Manny locked the door and bolted it behind them. She sat down on the edge of one of the two beds and let the bag slide to the floor at her feet. "So what now?"

"We'll catch the earliest flight I can book to D.C. I didn't want to hang out at the airport. It's too open, and we'd be visible for too long."

"So we just sit here in the meantime."

"Yes. You can take a shower if you want," he offered. "I have clothes for you in the car."

She looked up in surprise.

"You asked for clothes when you were in the hospital. You just didn't stick around long enough to collect them," he said pointedly.

"Thank you," she murmured. "I'll go climb in now." The mere thought of a shower made her positively weak-kneed. She needed to fix her hair color anyway.

Once inside, she stripped off her jeans and shirt, wincing at the vivid bruises across her abdomen and chest. She made the mistake of looking into the mirror and gasped at her reflection. In a word, she looked bloody awful. The dye job looked cheap, and deep shadows marked her eyes.

She pulled out her supplies, lined them on the counter and then stepped into the shower. She turned on the water as hot as she could make it and stuck her head underneath the spray.

Manuel waited until he heard the flow of water before he relaxed his guard. He needed to call Tony and get the flight information...and any other information Tony had been able to dig up.

He took out his phone and began the arduous task of routing his call through the backup network, one Tony himself had devised. A few moments later, Tony's low voice came over the line.

"I've got your flight info. Bad news is, I couldn't get you a flight until tomorrow morning even with pulling strings. The weather in Chicago has the afternoon schedule a complete cluster fuck. I would have booked a flight, but I wasn't sure about Jules's reservation. You need to see if she has any ID, because if she doesn't, you're both fucked. You also need to use one of your aliases. Sanderson would know in a minute if you booked the flight as Manuel Ramirez."

Manuel sighed. "I have no idea. She's in the shower now, but I'll check on it when she gets out, then I'll get back to you so you can make the reservations. You find out anything else?" He held his breath as he asked the question.

"Not yet. Hopefully by the time you get here."

Manuel thanked him and hung up, letting out a long breath. He felt so goddamn guilty about deceiving Sanderson. The man had been very understanding of Manuel's need to find Jules. He'd turned the other way countless times when Manuel had used department resources. And now Manuel was not only lying to him, but he was indulging in activity that could very well brand him as a traitor.

What a goddamn mess. But what choice did he have? He couldn't hang Jules out to dry, no matter what she'd done. *And if she's a traitor?* God, he couldn't bring himself to consider the sweet, innocent girl he'd loved forever could possibly have joined a fucking terrorist group. No matter how damning the evidence.

He ran a hand through his hair in agitation. They still needed to talk. But first he had to get her clothes.

He slipped out of the room and hurried out to the car to retrieve the bag in the back seat. When he walked back into the room, he nearly collided with Jules as she came out of the bathroom.

He swallowed hard as he took in her damp body wrapped in just a towel. Averting his gaze, he held out the bag to her. "Here are your clothes."

"Thank you," she said shortly. "I'll be a bit with my hair." Then she retreated back into the bathroom.

He crossed the room and folded his large frame into the armchair by the window. How had things gotten so damn complicated? He had more questions than ever, but the one foremost on his mind was whether she'd planned to join the NFR even before she had left for France. Or was her traveling there just a huge coincidence?

He rubbed his eyes. He needed sleep. They both needed sleep. But most of all he needed answers. Real answers. How in the world could he get her to talk? She had flatly refused to tell him much beyond admitting her association with the NFR. If it was a simple matter of trust, he might be hurt that she wouldn't confide in him, but he sensed it was more than that. She was trying to protect him, and that pissed him off more than her holding back.

He must have dozed for a while. He opened his eyes when he heard the bathroom door open. Jules padded out in the pair of jeans and T-shirt he had provided her. Her hair was brushed behind her ears, still damp, but the red was gone, replaced by pale blonde.

The T-shirt did nothing to disguise her thinness and appearance of fragility. It was hard to reconcile those with the images of her disabling the guard at the hospital and shooting the assassins from the cabin.

She sat on the edge of the bed and stared ahead for a long while before finally glancing over to where he sat.

"I need to make flight reservations," he said, breaking the silence. "I'm assuming you have multiple forms of identification."

She nodded. Bending over, she pulled several passports from her bag and spread them out on the bed. "We're flying to D.C., right?"

He nodded.

"And are we supposed to have a relationship or are we flying separately?"

He arched an eyebrow. "Together."

"Stupid question," she muttered.

"Yeah, it was. You aren't getting out of my sight."

She flipped him a Maryland driver's license. "Then I suppose I'll be her."

He picked it up, studying the picture and the name. Christina Maxwell. He glanced back up at her, wondering just how close she had been to him during the last three years.

As if reading his thoughts, she shook her head. "I've never set foot in Maryland."

He picked up his phone and dialed Tony. After relaying the information to him, he hung up. "Our flight is at eight tomorrow morning."

Relief spread across her tired face. The shadows had grown longer under her eyes, and fatigue was etched deeply into her every movement.

"Why don't you crawl into bed while I take a shower," he said gently.

She said nothing. He sensed she was too exhausted to speak. He got up and walked into the bathroom but left the door open so he could see the room door clearly.

Jules pulled herself to her feet as soon as she heard the shower go on. Retrieving her bag from the floor, she poured the contents out on the bed. Currency from five countries was bound in stacks of bills. Six passports, all sporting different identities, spilled out. The Glock and HK 94 gleamed in the soft lamplight, and she experienced a moment of panic. They would have to be left behind.

Ammunition and countless maps littered the spread. Her small GPS unit lay to the side, but her focus was on the cell phone lying in the middle of the pile. Her hand reached out to touch it tentatively. She knew he'd tried to call. Would continue to call until she turned it on. He wasn't someone who gave up.

Her stomach curling with nausea, she pressed the power button. Silence loomed, and she breathed a sigh of relief. She let it fall back to the bed and began gathering the items she would take with her the next day.

Out of the corner of her eye, she saw the phone's screen light up. Then it pulsed and vibrated, moving slightly. Bile rose in her throat. She stared at it then glanced toward the bathroom. The water still ran, steam pouring from the stall.

As if it were a venomous snake, she reached for the phone with a cautious hand, her dread increasing as her fingers closed around it.

Taking a deep breath, she snatched it up and punched a button. "What do you want?"

Northstar's sarcastic sneer filtered through the line. "Ahh, so you did escape the NFR's clumsy attempt to take you out."

She closed her eyes. "You don't need me anymore. Why won't you just let me go?"

"Oh, but I do need you, Magalie. One last time."

"There will never be a last time," she retorted. "I'm not stupid."

"I have a proposition for you. One that is beneficial to us both, but even more so for you."

"Just get to the point." She glanced toward the bathroom. "I don't have much time."

"I have an assignment for you. Should be nothing for a woman of your talents. If you complete it, you're free to go. What you do with the rest of your life is of no consequence to me."

"And if I refuse?"

His voice changed from the baiting tone he'd been using to one of complete ruthlessness. "If you refuse, you can kiss your little boyfriend goodbye. Don't fuck with me. You know what I'm capable of. Removing lover boy from the picture would be nothing more than swatting an insect with a flyswatter."

Jules's heart leaped into her throat. Yes, she knew he was serious. Killing people was what he did. He would kill his own mother for effect. He had killed *her* parents in a demonstration of his power. She had to protect Manny. At all costs. "How do I know you won't keep dangling him in front of me when this mission is over? What guarantee do I have that you're telling the truth?"

"You have none, and I'm not offering any. I have no further use for you. Assassins like you are a dime a dozen. I have no wish to continue babysitting you through your tantrums. Do this assignment, and you'll have what you most want. Your freedom. Refuse and I'll make your life a living hell. Maybe you remember what happened the first time you hesitated."

Suffocating fear swept through her with alarming speed. Memories she tried hard to keep locked away in her mind fought to escape. Sweat broke out on her forehead. Damn him for what he'd done to her.

"Or maybe you liked it?" he taunted. "Did you enjoy it, Magalie?"

"I'll do it," she said quietly. Anything to get him to shut up. Make the horrible memories go away. She had to keep Manny safe and her tenuous grip on sanity in check.

"I thought you would see it my way," he said. "When you get to D.C., check your e-mail. I'll have detailed instructions for you."

"How did you know I was going to D.C.?" she demanded.

Silence greeted her question. "Damn it," she swore, throwing the phone down.

She began to pace in agitation. How could she do what she vowed she'd never do again? How could she *not* do it? Manny was everything to her. Could she trust Northstar to keep his word?

Of course she couldn't trust him, but she had no other choice than to comply with his directive. It was his careless discarding of her that gave her hope that he was through with her. He needed her now, but there was always someone waiting in the wings to take up the cause.

Sadness twisted in her chest. Manny wanted her to trust him, to hand everything over to him and let him take care of it. As tempting as the idea was in theory, the bastards he worked for made it an impossibility. By going to Manny with the truth, she'd be placing their lives in the very hands she fought to keep Manny *from*.

No, she'd have to pull on the cloak of the assassin one more time, or the people Manny trusted would end his life.

Her mind raced, analyzing the situation. In order to pull it off, she would have to convince Manny that he had won. He could in no way suspect that she would run or that she was planning the unthinkable. It would take the performance of her life.

No. She wouldn't lie to him. She would merely tell him the truth. The complete and utter truth. Her stomach lurched at the idea of ever speaking aloud the horrible images that haunted her every waking moment.

For the first time in three years, she would be completely honest with someone.

Her lip curled in distaste. Grief settled over her as she slowly began the transformation back into the person she hated most. The cold-blooded killer.

Chapter Eleven

When Manny stepped out of the bathroom, Jules's eyes riveted to him. Even as she tried to look away, she found she couldn't. He wore a pair of gym shorts, and his bare chest was damp. His dark hair was in disarray and wet. He crossed the room and picked up a folded shirt from the chair.

She watched, fascinated, as he raised his arms to pull the shirt over his head. Muscles rippled in his abdomen and chest, bulged and contorted in his arms. He lifted his gaze to hers as he let the shirt fall to his waist, and she flushed guiltily, embarrassed to have been caught staring.

"Are you hungry?" he asked, his gaze caressing her face, studying her. "I can call for takeout."

Her stomach rumbled in response. Though the thought of food made her feel sick, she knew it was because she hadn't eaten in so long. The few bites of the pancakes Manny had made for her had settled like stones in her stomach. She nodded. "Sounds good."

"Any preference?" he asked as he flipped through the thick phonebook.

"No, you choose." Her stomach heaved again as she considered how she could possibly pull off what Northstar wanted her to do.

Manny picked up the phone and called in a delivery order for sandwiches and drinks then hung up. He turned to her, his expression determined. "I want to have a look at your injuries. You shouldn't even be out of the hospital, much less running all over the damned country."

She scooted back on the bed in alarm. This she hadn't counted on. He stood over her, his expression neutral. "Just lie back. This won't take long."

Gingerly, she reclined on the bed, and his fingers gently pulled up her shirt to bare her stomach. He frowned as he looked down at her chest. "Jesus, Jules. You look like you got in a fight with Easter egg dye."

"Thanks," she muttered.

His fingers probed and ran lightly over her belly and out over her ribs. She hissed in pain when he hit a particularly tender spot.

"I'm sorry, baby," he said, his eyes full of regret. "Does your head still hurt?"

"Right now, there isn't too much of me that doesn't hurt," she said truthfully.

He frowned. "I have some Tylenol in my bag. I want you to take some."

He dug out two pills then filled a plastic cup with water and handed them both to her. He watched as she downed the tablets in one swallow then took the cup back from her. "Rest until the food gets here," he ordered.

Not about to argue, she leaned back into the pillows, her eyes closing. It felt good to let Manny take care of her. Even if it was only temporary.

Manuel watched as Jules sank into the bed, her eyes fluttering closed. She looked beyond exhausted. Pale, fragile. Like she could break at any moment.

How much had she sacrificed for Mom and Pop? For him? He wished he had the full story. He sat there for several minutes watching the rise and fall of her chest. A knock on the door startled him momentarily. Jules's eyes flew open in alarm, and he put a finger to his lips.

"Food," he mouthed silently at her.

She nodded but kept her eyes trained on him as he drew his gun and walked cautiously to the door. He peered out the peephole to see a young guy, no more than a teenager, standing in the hallway.

Not taking any chances, he called out, "Set the food down. I'm sliding a twenty under the door. You can keep the change."

The boy didn't so much as blink an eye. He plopped the food down then collected the bill Manuel stuffed under the door. "Thanks, mister," he called before hurrying back down the hall.

Manuel waited several moments then carefully opened the door and stuck his head out. Seeing the hall empty, he bent down to retrieve the sack and the two drinks.

He carried them back inside and set the sack down on the end of Jules's bed. She sat up and hungrily eyed the sandwiches he was unwrapping.

"I got you chicken salad and root beer," he said, allowing himself a small grin.

She let out a groan of sheer ecstasy. "Root beer. Oh my God."

He chuckled and tossed her the can. Then he handed over her sandwich and collected the bag. He moved to the small table by the window and unwrapped his own food.

They ate in silence. Jules seemed to savor every bite, and he wondered, not for the first time, how long she had gone without meals in the past.

He checked his watch when he finished. Though he was aching for answers to his questions, he knew Jules needed rest more than anything. And he could use a night's sleep himself.

He stripped off his shirt then walked over to the bed closest to the window and pulled back the covers. He could feel Jules looking at him as he slid beneath the sheets. Turning in her direction, he propped his head up with his hand and watched her while she finished eating.

With a nervous glance in his direction, she tossed her can in the garbage beside the bed and stood up. He averted his eyes while she slipped out of her jeans, but he could see her slim legs, her shirt falling to mid-thigh.

To his surprise she moved closer to him until she stood directly over him. He looked up to see her blue eyes wide, uncertainty shining in their midst. "Do you remember when I used to crawl into bed with you and we'd talk?"

His chest swelled, memories burning brightly. They had talked for hours until she fell asleep. He had savored those moments of closeness with her. He scooted over and patted the spot next to him, wondering if she wanted to do that now.

She slid in beside him, and he pulled the covers over her slight form. He reached his hand out to gently caress her face, his fingers trailing down her cheek then up over her ear to tuck a blonde curl away.

"Don't try to hide from me again, Jules. Whatever's out there, we can face it together."

She looked away. "I won't run again."

Triumph surged through his veins. He stared at her for a long moment, trying to decide whether or not to bring up the subject of her disappearance. He didn't want to push her, but she seemed to be waiting expectantly. Did she want him to ask? "Do you want to talk?"

Fear leapt to her eyes as she turned back to him. "I-I..." Her voice trailed off, and she swallowed hard. "What do you want to know?"

"Why don't you start at the beginning?" he gently urged. "What happened in France? Why did you call me and tell me you couldn't be near me or Mom and Pop?"

She took in a shaky breath, and he rubbed his hand up and down her side, wanting her to feel secure.

"I was having coffee, waiting for the train back to Paris. It was the day before I was supposed to fly home." She rolled over on her back and stared at the ceiling. He let his hand fall away and watched her intently as she continued.

"A waiter delivered a drink from some guy at the bar. Next thing I know, a Frenchman sat down at my table and began spouting weird things."

"Like what?" Manuel asked.

"He told me my real name was Magalie Pinson and that my parents were Frederic and Carine Pinson. I told him he was psycho, that my name was Jules Trehan and I'd never heard of the Pinsons."

Manuel frowned. So far this wasn't just weird, it was plain bizarre.

"He then said that they had killed my real parents."

"Who did?"

"He didn't say," she replied. "He handed me an envelope and told me when I'd read the contents to give him a call, that we had much to discuss, including my future."

"What was in the envelope?" he asked, unable to remain silent. A thousand questions were burning a trail through his brain. None of this made any sense.

"I didn't read it until much later. It was recruitment information for the NFR, and it gave detailed information about my supposed parents. They were members of the NFR's charter group."

"And you believed them?" he asked in disbelief. This didn't sound like the Jules he knew. She wasn't so gullible.

Her eyes flashed angrily. "Of course I didn't believe it. I told him to take a hike. He walked away. Then the guy from the bar walked over, pulled a gun and told me to come with him. He was American, to my surprise, and he told me it was time for me to find out who I really was. He shoved me into a taxi, and we took off."

"And what then?"

She paused for a long time, staring up at the ceiling, her breath coming in short bursts. "And then I went to hell."

He shoved up on his elbow and curled an arm around her waist, forcing her to turn slightly toward him. "You're with me now, Jules. They can't hurt you anymore."

"I wish I could believe that."

"Talk to me," he asked, not sure how hard to push her. But he needed the truth. Needed to know why she had agreed to do the unthinkable. "Why can't you believe that I can protect you?"

She appeared to think deeply about his question. She went completely still, and her breathing shallowed. She seemed to be fighting a very personal battle, one she wasn't sure she wanted to share with him.

He held his breath, not realizing until now just how important it was to him that she trusted him.

"The man asked me if I intended to join the NFR. Of course, I hadn't even opened the envelope. Didn't plan to. I had no idea what he was talking about, so I told him no way in hell. Then I told him what he could do with his questions."

Manuel almost smiled. He could well imagine that scene.

"He didn't appreciate my colorful language. The taxi stopped outside the town we'd been in, and he forced me into another car. He tied my hands and blindfolded me. We drove forever."

She closed her eyes, her sadness and fear reaching out to him as if he were a lifeline. Reaching for her hand, he laced his fingers through hers and squeezed reassuringly.

"When we stopped, he made me get out, and we walked into a building. He took the blindfold off and left the room. It looked just like any office complex. We were in the city. I could tell by the traffic noises. I could hear copy machines and telephones ringing. There were other people in the building, and I contemplated screaming to get their attention. The man, Northstar as I later came to know him, walked back in before I could. The way he looked at me was frightening. So cold. I was really afraid for the first time.

"He explained that I'd been approached by a member of the NFR based on my parents' prior relationship with the group. When I told him I had no intention of joining any sort of a group, he laughed at me. Then he told me I had no choice in the matter.

"I told him to screw off, and he pulled an envelope from a desk. He handed it to me and told me to look inside. When I did I saw pictures of Mom and Pop...and you," she said, choking as she got the words out. "I still didn't understand. To me you were a world away, out of this maniac's reach. He then told me that unless I did exactly as he instructed he would have you all killed."

Manuel bit the inside of his lip in anger.

"I know what you're thinking." She scooted up in the bed. "And believe me, I had the same thoughts. I figured I'd agree to anything, then I'd go to the police or the American embassy as fast as I could. And he must have figured out what I was thinking. He asked me point-blank if I thought he was serious, and in my stupidity, I said I didn't know.

"He pressed a button on his desk and called a woman into the room. She looked like a secretary. When she walked in, he pulled out a gun and shot her in the head. Right there in front of me!" She wrapped her arms around her legs hugged them tightly to her chest.

"Mother of God," Manuel muttered. He sat up and pulled her stiff body into his arms.

She stuck her arms in front of her, preventing him from holding her close. She fidgeted away from him, looking past him, through him with glassy eyes.

"He asked if I believed him then, and all I could do was nod. I was in shock. There was blood everywhere. And then—then—" She broke off, her voice cracking.

"Then what?" he prompted softly.

"Another man walked in. He was older. Distinguished-looking, actually. He never spoke. He just smiled. Then he raped me right there by the dead body. I was so in shock I couldn't even fight him."

Pure unadulterated rage boiled over Manuel. He clenched and unclenched his fingers in rapid succession. Then he pulled her close, ignoring her attempts to keep distance between them.

He rocked her back and forth in his arms, stroking her hair, her back, every inch of her he could touch. He felt in danger of losing his mind. Red crowded his vision. He'd never been so close to the desire to kill anyone before in his life, and yet if he could get his hands on the bastard who had hurt her, he'd derive great pleasure from making him bleed from every orifice of his body.

She lay lifeless in his arms. He closed his eyes and held on to her.

"When he was finished, he left me lying there on the floor," she said, her voice muffled by Manny's chest. He eased his hold on her to allow her more room.

"He told Northstar to take care of it. It was then I knew he was also American. After he left, Northstar took the picture of Mom and Pop and smeared the woman's blood on it. Then he dropped it on the floor next to me and told me that if I ever had any doubts that he was serious, to look at the picture and remember whose blood was on it. He ordered me to get up and clean myself. Then he held the phone while I told the Frenchman who'd first approached me about the NFR that I was interested in joining.

"The next day, I met with him and joined the organization," she said baldly. "Every month, Northstar sent me a new picture of Mom and Pop. It was always smeared with blood. I never found out who the man was who raped me, but I know he was in charge."

"God," Manuel whispered. What kind of hell had she endured? Her story was staggering. These kinds of things just didn't happen in her world. In his they did. He was used to the twisted things terrorists did to achieve their means. But what must it have been like for a naive girl of twenty-two?

She was as stiff as a board in his arms, almost as if she couldn't bear him touching her. He pulled her away, trying to find a comfortable position for her. Then he saw the shame in her eyes, the agony and the fear of his rejection.

"Jules, whatever you're thinking, don't." He cupped her chin in his hand and rubbed his thumb over her cheek, smoothing the tear-roughened skin. "If you think any of this affects the way I feel about you, baby...you couldn't be more wrong."

"But I've done things, Manny. Things I can't even speak of," she whispered in a tortured voice. "Every time I went out on a mission, I carried those pictures of Mom and Pop with me. I imagined you dead. Lifeless. And then I told myself that the only way to prevent the people I loved from paying for my mistakes was to do my job. So I traded someone else's life for yours. God, I hate myself for those decisions. I hated myself for feeling guilty over keeping my family alive."

More than ever, she looked like a lost little girl. Reminiscent of the toddler he'd found on the street so many years ago. The torture in her cloudy blue eyes was stark. Compelling. Very real.

He could well imagine what she'd been forced to do in the last three years. According to Tony, she'd gotten damn good at her job. He remembered her earlier statement that she wished she had just messed up a job and died. He knew now she'd been deadly serious. The weight of her burdens must have been unbearable.

"I'll help you, Jules. If you'll let me. Together we can get through this." He felt useless. Could he turn his back on the misdeeds she'd performed? Misdeeds. He made it sound like she had offended someone. Dead people couldn't be offended.

She shook her head vehemently. "Manny, no. You don't understand."

"Have you forgotten who I work for?" He forced her chin upwards so she looked at him. "I'm not without resources. I probably know more about the NFR than you do."

Jules's stomach twisted into a knot. There was too much Manny didn't know about her situation. He couldn't know everything. But what if he did? That scared the hell out of her. She wanted to trust him, believe in him completely. But how could she when he worked for the agency that controlled her fate?

She didn't dread death as she had in the beginning. Her fear of her own mortality had faded in the wake of so much pain and terror.

A slow burn radiated over her cheeks as Manny's gaze bored into her. He missed nothing. He could probably reach right into her thoughts and pluck one out at will. The CIA had chosen well when they'd recruited him. His sense of honor and duty made him a solid patriot.

Though she had told him things she'd never told another human being, things she'd kept locked deep within her, she felt no relief. She would've preferred he never know of the humiliation she'd suffered. She felt dirty and used. No better than a piece of trash someone had discarded. But they hadn't even thrown her away. How she wished they had. Then she could have crawled home and licked her wounds.

Instead, she'd embarked on a life she hated. No, it wasn't a life. It was an existence. She functioned. She'd given up living a long time ago.

Manny's hand slid around her neck and massaged the nape gently. His eyes glowed with concern, love, all the things she didn't deserve. Right now she hated herself more than ever before. Not even killing someone in cold blood could be worse than plotting to betray this man.

"Where are you, baby?"

She ducked her head guiltily. She should just ditch Manny and get to D.C. on her own. Being so close to him was only going to bring him greater attention from the people trying to kill her. Could she live with herself if she caused his death? The answer was a categorical no. She'd already killed her parents. And who cared if they were her real parents or not? They'd loved her like a daughter. She'd loved them.

"Jules? Are you okay?" Manny sounded worried now.

She stared up at him, trying to summon a reassuring smile, but she couldn't smile when all she felt was overwhelming grief. "No," she said honestly. "I'm not. I'm not sure I'll ever be okay."

He framed her face in his hands, and her heart lurched as he lowered his lips to hers. Her chest began to pound in a steady cadence, and she was robbed of breath. With infinite tenderness, he brushed his lips across hers. He was so gentle it made her want to weep. He held her like a piece of glass, one that might shatter with the slightest untoward movement.

She leaned hungrily into him, not caring that she intended to take his trust and trample it. All that mattered was that he kept on touching her. She could feel, really feel, for the first time in a long time.

His tongue laved across her lips, seeking entrance. Instantly, they parted, and he probed inward, lightly, delicately. One hand delved into her hair to the back of her head, coaxing her closer to him, as if trying to fuse their souls together.

"I should have died," she whispered against his lips. "It should have been me. Not Mom and Pop." She choked on the upsurge of grief.

"No. *No.*" He was a mere inch from her lips, his breath blowing hot over her face. Emotion knotted his voice. "Don't say it, Jules. I couldn't bear it if I lost you. You have no idea the hell I endured when you disappeared."

He kissed her temple then her cheek, and finally he reclaimed her lips with a light, tender kiss.

She felt the stirrings deep within, the faint whisper of something she desperately needed. Wanted. But couldn't have. The thought threw a wet blanket over her, and she pulled slowly away.

She drew in a steadying breath, trying to regain control of her desires. She felt exhausted by the myriad of emotions she'd experienced in rapid succession. It would be the easiest thing in the world to melt in his arms and see where the night would take them. But she wouldn't use Manny more than she already was.

"Go to sleep, baby." Manny pulled her down beside him and tucked the cover over them both.

She knew she should return to her own bed, but she couldn't deny herself the comfort of his embrace. Snuggling deep into his arms, she laid her head on his chest, closed her eyes and prayed for sleep to come.

Chapter Twelve

Manuel stood by the bed watching Jules sleep. She was curled up in a ball like a kitten. He wanted to reach out and touch her but didn't want to disturb her. Perhaps sleep was the only time she could escape the horrors that haunted her.

How had things become such a mess? Years ago, all he had wanted was a normal life. Marry Jules, have a few kids, live the American dream. Even his recruitment into the CIA didn't hinder his goals. He'd dedicate a few years to Uncle Sam then go on to more normal pursuits.

Instead he'd been locked in a never-ending nightmare. The difficulties facing him and Jules seemed insurmountable. He wasn't naive, and he wasn't an eternal optimist. He had no clear idea how he was going to extricate them from this cluster fuck.

The NFR was obviously pissed enough to want to take her out, and if the U.S. government ever found out about her involvement, much less the things she'd done during her years with a known terrorist organization, they'd throw her under the jail.

In this climate, terrorists weren't tolerated at all. You didn't even so much as hint that you were sympathetic to such causes or you'd draw the ever-omnipotent eye of Big Brother.

And where did that leave him? CIA agent aiding and abetting a known terrorist cell member. Jesus, it didn't even bear contemplating.

He checked his watch. They still had an hour before he needed to wake her so they could catch their flight. He walked into the bathroom to call Tony.

"I was just going to call you," Tony said.

"What's up?"

"I have the info you requested. NFR's recruitment tactics."

Manuel burned with anger over the mere mention of their *tactics*. They were no better than animals.

"They're pretty tame when compared to most radical groups," Tony continued on. "Basically their M.O. is to approach a subject, outline the group's objective, leave a way to contact them and disappear."

"What else?" Manuel asked.

"That's it. It's up to the individual to either contact or ignore the invitation. They aren't into forced recruitment. It doesn't make for loyal followers."

Bile rose in Manuel's throat. Had Jules lied to him? Had she taken him on the ride of his life? No, she wasn't that good. No way in hell that anguish had been feigned. "Are you sure you aren't mistaken, Tony?" he asked. "Are there any documented cases of more persuasive means?"

Silence fell over the line. "What are you saying, Manuel? Was Jules forced into the NFR?"

Manuel sighed. "I'm not sure what the hell I'm saying. Jules has a slightly different account of her induction into the NFR."

"You believe her?"

He paused. "Yeah, I do. Something doesn't add up. Her story matches what you said to a point. Some guy approached her in France. Fed her a bullshit line about who her real parents were then left her with an envelope and told her to call him the next day. Only that's where the similarities end."

"What do you mean, exactly? And what's the deal with the parents? Didn't you say the Trehans adopted her?"

Manuel frowned. He wasn't ready to tell Tony what had happened to Jules. Not until he was able to figure it out. The whole story. "Yeah, she was told her real parents were Frederic and Carine Pinson."

"Hmm. I'll do some checking. Maybe I can come up with something."

"Thank you, Tony. This just keeps getting more complicated."

"No problem. But Manuel, you need to be careful. If she's who you say she is, you're going to have to keep a low profile. The higher-ups already want you to bring her in. They've been looking for a line into the NFR for a long time now. They wouldn't hesitate to use her if they could. And if they couldn't...well you know what we do to terrorists."

"See what you can find out about the people the NFR has assassinated in the last three years," Manuel said. "I need to know everything I can about Jules's involvement."

"Will do," Tony promised. "Now get on the plane, and for God's sake, when you get to D.C., keep out of sight. Sanderson's about to have a coronary wondering where you are, and if he smells you in D.C. you'll be up shit creek without a paddle."

Manuel laughed. "Thanks for the heads-up, Tony. And thanks for helping me," he added after a long breath.

"Not even going to dignify that with a reply."

Manuel slid the phone back into his pocket. He walked into the bedroom, mulling over what Tony had related. Part of Jules's story made sense. But the rest was just plain bizarre.

He seethed imagining her at the mercy of the man who'd hurt her. He knew without a doubt she'd told him the truth. But... There was always a *but.* Had she told him the *whole* truth? Had she left out any part of the story?

He sat down on the edge of the bed, resting his hand on her head. Was she still trying to protect him? How could he get her to give up that absurd notion? Whatever she thought, he wasn't going to let her get herself killed just to save his ass. He wasn't some junior agent out for a joyride. He could take what the NFR could dish.

She stirred, rustling the covers. A soft moan escaped her lips, and he stroked her hair, wanting so badly to take her in his arms and keep her there. Her eyes fluttered open, and for a moment, she looked confused and very much afraid. Then she smiled a slow, sleepy smile, relief pouring over her face.

Unable to help himself, he leaned over and kissed her soft, delectable lips. "Good morning."

Jules savored the feel of his lips, his touch rapidly dispelling the tenuous grip her nightmares held her in. As he drew away, she shifted, feeling a throbbing in her shoulder.

Frowning, she sat up and flexed her arm, rotating it around. Fleeting images assailed her mind. Memories of being drugged, held down, a hand in her hair, shoving her face into a pillow, searing pain in her shoulder, soft laughter above her. She squeezed her eyes shut, wanting them to go away. She hadn't analyzed those events since that awful day in France, choosing to shove the brutal memories to the far recesses of her mind. Only now that she had recounted them to Manny, they burned brightly in her head.

"Jules, are you all right?" Manny reached out to stroke her cheek and she flinched away.

The skin burned on her shoulder, the ache intensifying. She reached back, trying to remember the significance. So much of that day had been buried. Northstar, yanking her to her feet, telling her to clean herself up. Who was the other man? The one who'd raped her. Their voices intertwined in her head, both evil. She dug her fingers into her temples, desperate to make the pain go away.

Who *was* he? She tried to picture him, but all she could feel was pain, overwhelming fear. *Wait.* She'd seen him one other time. During her training. God, those days were fuzzy, a mixture of pain and humiliation. She'd been shoved facedown on the couch, someone straddling her body. Voices in the background, *his* voice, instructing. Searing pain in her shoulder, nausea welling up in her throat. Something cold poured over her skin. Then blackness. Nothing. She couldn't remember.

"Jules!" Manny's voice was firmer this time.

She struggled from the darkness closing around her. Her breath came rapidly, and then she knew she was going to be sick.

She bolted from the bed, shoving Manny aside. She raced to the bathroom and lunged for the toilet. No sooner had she stumbled to the floor than her stomach lurched and heaved.

Strong hands encircled her waist, picked her up and locked her to Manny's side. He helped her bend over as she heaved violently, his hands never loosening their hold.

His fingers stroked back her hair as he waited for her to finish. He didn't speak, and she was grateful for the silence. Her head couldn't take the slightest noise at the moment.

When her turmoil subsided, she slumped weakly against him, wiping the back of her mouth with her hand. He left her for a moment, and she heard the trickle of water. A second later, he handed her a plastic cup so she could rinse her mouth out. Then, without a word, he swept her into his arms. He tucked her head under his chin and just held her.

He walked back into the bedroom and sat on the edge of the bed, pulling her even closer to him until there was no space between them. Silence settled over the room, so much so that she could hear her own heart beating. It pounded wildly in her chest, and she was sure he could feel the thundering against his body.

But still he said nothing. Gradually she began to relax in his arms, until she sagged limply against him. The burning in her shoulder intensified though, and she could smell blood. Her blood. Was it a memory? What had they done to her? They'd stripped her of all dignity, but it hadn't been enough. Would it ever be enough?

She shifted to relieve the discomfort in her back. Manny loosened his hold, and she eased away from him. She kept her eyes downcast, not wanting to see anything reflected in his gaze. Pity. No, she didn't want to see pity there. The last thing she wanted was for Manny to feel sorry for her.

"I'm going to go take a shower," she mumbled.

She stumbled back into the bathroom and turned the shower on full force. After stripping away her clothing, she stepped under the icy spray, gasping as her body numbed. She forced herself to remain under the cold, needing the shock to clear her head. She had to get it together. Where was the calculating assassin when she needed her?

After several more minutes of self-punishment, she stepped from the shower and toweled herself off. She stood naked in front of the mirror, staring at her reflection. She tried hardening her features, her eyes, anything to regain the tough shell she'd worked so hard to perfect. But all she saw was a fragile, scared mouse.

The tingling in her shoulder nagged her until finally she turned around, looking back over her shoulder into the mirror. But all she saw was the small tattoo Northstar had forced her to get. Was that what she was remembering?

She shook her head in confusion. No, she distinctly remembered getting the tattoo, but the other images made no sense. The tattoo, while uncomfortable, wasn't that painful. The things she remembered—her blood, the painful cutting—weren't from the tattoo. But it felt like the same spot. That whole period was one long, drug-induced haze.

Maybe she was missing something. She contorted her body to once again look in the mirror but saw nothing but the coiled snake stamped on her shoulder.

Looking in the mirror had not been something she spent time doing in the last three years. Her entire back could be painted purple and she wouldn't know it. She turned back around, wondering if she should ask Manny to check it out.

He'd think she was nuts. Probably already did.

She thrust her arms into a simple T-shirt, not bothering to put on a bra. Then she collected the jeans Manny had bought for her and pulled them on over her still-damp legs. Even though Houston was a great deal warmer than Colorado and New Mexico, she put on the warm-up jacket and zipped it partway up. It gave her the appearance of added protection, even if it was only an illusion.

She glanced back in the mirror. "Don't screw this up, Jules," she said fiercely. "Stop acting like a ninny and get with the program."

She stood there, staring at her determined reflection until she felt some of the uncertainty melt away. She was doing this for Manny. For the parents she'd failed. For them, she could set aside the paralyzing terror and shame.

Finally satisfied that she'd put herself back together, she opened the door and stepped into the bedroom.

Manuel immediately noticed the change in Jules. Gone was the terrified, shaken angel, and in her place stood a composed, confident woman.

She met his gaze, her eyes coolly assessing him. Her stance was almost arrogant, and her attitude was take-charge. "Are all the arrangements made?"

He nodded, at a loss as to how to handle this change in her. "Our flight leaves in an hour and a half so we need to get going."

She nodded and collected her bag. She took out her Glock and the HK 94, checking to see that both were loaded. She jammed a new magazine into place and engaged the safety. It was obvious she knew her way around firearms, and it made him damned uncomfortable. He didn't need reminders of the way she'd lived for the last few years.

"You can't take those with you," he said, folding his arms across his chest.

Her lip curled. "You think? Gee, I didn't know that."

He raised an eyebrow. "So what are you doing with them, then?"

"Making sure we get to the airport in one piece," she muttered. "I assume you have a drop-off point for your Beamer? I mean, it wouldn't do for the average pencil-necked security guard to get his hands on the Bondmobile." Sarcasm dripped heavily from her voice. "I'll leave the guns with the car. The rest goes with me."

He almost laughed. Until he remembered why she was working so hard to put on a strong front. His gut tightened. "The Bondmobile gets dropped off outside the airport perimeter. We'll take a shuttle in."

She finished shoving her stuff in then slung the too-large bag over her thin shoulder. She looked up at him, her eyes reminding him of iron prison bars. Impenetrable.

"Let's go then," she announced, looking like she was ready to take on the world.

He didn't like that look. It gave him the distinct impression she was up to something that would turn his world upside-down. More than it already was.

Chapter Thirteen

Manuel maneuvered the BMW onto the beltway and accelerated into the middle lane. Jules leaned back in the seat, her expression stoic. What he wouldn't give to know what was going on in that head of hers. And then again, maybe he was better off not knowing.

He changed lanes in anticipation of the upcoming exit. Traffic had eased as the morning rush hour was abating. As he slowed to get off the beltway, the car lurched crazily forward, snapping his head back against the seat.

"What the—?"

Jules recovered quickly and twisted around. "That son of a bitch hit us!"

Manuel checked the rearview mirror just in time to see the grille of a Hummer ram into their back bumper again.

Jules swore loud and long.

"Anyone ever tell you what a potty mouth you have?"

She glared at him and climbed halfway over the back of the seat.

"What the hell are you doing?" he demanded as he accelerated and veered over two lanes in an attempt to shake their pursuer.

"Making sure those assholes don't kill us." She hauled her Glock out of her bag and rolled her window down.

He reached over and yanked the hood of her jacket back, causing her to tumble toward him. "Use your head, damn it. You can't have a shootout in the middle of Houston."

She glared at him. "Who said anything about a shootout?" She scrambled forward once more and leaned out the window. Taking careful aim, she squeezed off two rounds.

Manuel saw the Hummer sway erratically and skid to the side. She'd blown out both front tires. He jammed his foot to the accelerator and surged forward.

The Hummer recovered and stayed close behind the BMW as Manuel weaved in and out of traffic.

"We've got company," Jules muttered.

He looked in his rearview mirror and swore. Two sets of flashing lights were closing on them.

"Look out!"

He yanked the steering wheel to avoid a truck merging from the on-ramp. He shot around it and dove off the upcoming exit. He needed to get off the highway and fast.

He slowed to turn on a side street and the Hummer rammed them from behind again, spinning the BMW around a hundred and eighty degrees. Never taking his foot off the gas, he righted the wheel and kept going.

"Why aren't they slowing down, damn it? I took out their front tires." She leaned out and fired another shot. This time they shot back.

"Get back in here," he barked, yanking on her jacket.

His side-view mirror exploded. "Son of a bitch!" He fishtailed into another curve and barreled down a side street.

No matter what he did, he couldn't shake the other vehicle. And the cops were right behind them.

"Hold on," he muttered through his teeth. He slammed on the brakes as the Hummer came up beside them. Jerking the wheel, he executed a perfect J-turn and immediately accelerated in the opposite direction.

Only problem was, the cops were bearing down on them, and unless he rammed them, the only alternative was to stop. A quick glance in the mirror told him the Hummer had split.

"Shit." He jammed his foot on the brake and came to a complete stop as cop cars converged from every direction. "Don't do anything stupid," he warned, not sure what Jules would do when threatened with capture.

She gave him a nasty look and immediately stuck her hands out the window. He did the same, and soon cops were yanking them out of the car.

He was bent over the hood, his hands twisted behind him as two officers cuffed him. He looked up to see Jules slammed on the hood, her face against the metal as her arms were wrenched behind her back. "Watch it," he snarled. "There's no need to get rough with her."

"Shut the hell up," the cop closest to his ear hissed. "What the hell did you think you were doing? Having it out with an opposing gang?"

"Do I look like a gangbanger?" Manuel growled as he was hauled upright.

He and Jules were read their rights then unceremoniously stuffed into two separate cruisers. He watched the car with her in it glide away. Damn it all to hell. This was not what he needed. Though he doubted he had anything to worry about, he hoped like hell Jules kept in character and did no talking.

When they arrived at the station house, he was fingerprinted and took the prerequisite mug shot. Before they could so much as ask him a question, he insisted on his phone call.

"My phone," he snarled at the cop who'd manhandled Jules.

The man slapped the phone into Manuel's hand and stood to the side as Manuel punched in Tony's number. Please don't let this be the one time he was standing down.

"I guess this means you didn't catch your flight," Tony said wearily as he answered.

"How'd you know?"

"You should be in the air right now. You're on your phone. So you aren't."

"Got it in one," he muttered. "I need a favor, man. And I need it yesterday." He quickly outlined what had happened. "I need to get Jules out of here before anyone starts asking questions, and before Sanderson gets wind that we've been picked up."

"Nothing's ever easy with you." Tony sounded exasperated.

"Can you get me out of here or not?"

"Give me a few minutes. Hang tight."

Manuel hung up the phone and handed it back to the policeman. "Take me to my cell, Danno."

"It's Officer Williams to you," the cop ground out.

He glared at the cop on his way by. He usually took a much more tolerant stance toward the local uniforms, but this one had crossed the line. "Like roughing up the women?"

"The woman was firing a weapon out the window of your car," Williams snarled.

Okay, he had a point, but it still didn't warrant the mistreatment Jules had undergone. Manuel compressed his lips into a thin line and entered the cell. The door clanged behind him, and he began to time how long it would take Tony to get his ass out of a crack this time.

And then he began to worry about Jules.

Ten minutes later, the cop returned and opened the cell door. "Why didn't you tell us who you were?"

Manuel raised an eyebrow. "And who am I?" he asked, wondering what story Tony had come up with.

"Damn feds. Arrogant sons of bitches."

Ahh, so Tony had made him an FBI agent. Just as well. The cops would be only too glad to see him gone. They tended to get territorial when the feds came sniffing around their turf.

He followed Williams to where Jules was being held in a cell block across the precinct. As they approached her cell, he could see her huddled in the far corner. She sat on the floor, her knees hunched to her chest. But when she saw him, she leaped up, all signs of vulnerability gone.

She stalked over to the bars and glared at the cop. Then she turned her attention to Manuel. "We getting out?"

In answer to her question, Williams slid the cell door open. She glided through the opening, and with a satisfied smirk, stepped on the cop's toe. He grimaced and shot her a glare.

"The lieutenant wants to see you before you leave," Williams said. His distaste was obvious. He clearly wanted them to be gone immediately.

Manuel put a hand to Jules's back and led her down the hall after the officer. They walked into a small office, and a fortyish-looking man scowled at them over the rim of his glasses.

"Sit down," he ordered, taking off his glasses and dropping them on his desk.

Jules complied but Manuel stood, opting to lean against the bookcase that lined the wall. He wasn't one to give up any advantage.

"What the hell are you doing here?" the lieutenant asked. Manuel glanced at the nameplate toward the front of the desk.

"'Fraid I can't tell you that, Lieutenant Barnes."

"Bullshit. You idiots were shooting up my streets." He glared over at Jules as he spoke.

She stiffened, and Manuel willed her to remain silent.

"I have no idea why they wanted to kill us," Manuel responded evenly. "But my partner had no desire to see them succeed."

The lieutenant let out a string of expletives that singed Manuel's ears. "Get the hell out of here. Get on I-10 and don't look back. I don't want to get so much as a hint of you coming back to Houston."

"We need a ride," Manuel pointed out, trying not to piss the lieutenant off further.

"And I want my stuff back," Jules said in a steely voice. "All of it."

"Ask Williams to give you a ride to impound. As for your stuff, sign for it at the desk," Barnes said with a grunt.

Manuel and Jules left the lieutenant's office to see Williams leaning against the wall. "Come on. I haven't got all day."

They followed him out to his cruiser and slid into the back. "I think I've had enough of back seats for a while," Jules muttered.

"Let's just hope the Bondmobile is drivable."

"You mean it's not indestructible?"

"Cut the sarcasm."

"Here you are," Williams announced, roaring into the impound lot. "Check with McKilheny over there. He'll get the keys for you."

No sooner had Manuel and Jules stepped out of the car than Williams peeled away.

"I can feel the love," Jules drawled.

"Let's get going."

A few minutes later, the two of them stood and surveyed the damage done to the Beamer. The back end was pretty much toast, but it should get them where they were going.

Jules slid into the passenger seat and waited as Manny got in on the driver's side. She was wound as tight as a rubber band at full stretch. All her instincts screamed that something was wrong. And not just the fact someone had tried to make road pizza out of them.

She leaned her head back as Manny drove out of the lot.

"You okay?" Manny asked, glancing over at her.

"Yeah. Just thinking."

"About?"

She remained silent for a long time. If she confided her suspicions, he'd think she was nuts. She wasn't sure she *wasn't* nuts. But nothing was adding up.

"Jules? Care to share?"

"Pull over somewhere," she said with a sigh. "This might take a while."

He pulled into a shopping center parking lot and stopped the engine. "What's bugging you? Besides the fact your former colleagues are trying to kill us."

"That's just it. They weren't from the NFR."

"Say that again?"

"You heard me."

"I see, and how did you discern they weren't NFR? Maybe they don't like driving Hummers?"

"Cut the sarcasm, Manny. I know what I'm talking about."

"Well, you see, Jules, my question isn't whether or not they're the NFR. My question is how they seem to know where we are no matter where we go. I find the coincidences to be staggering."

Her shoulder began aching in earnest, and she flexed it, rubbing her back in an attempt to ease the burning. Her memory nagged at her. She knew there was something important she was missing, but she couldn't put the pieces together.

He was staring expectantly at her, waiting for her to expound on her statement. "It's simply not something the NFR would do."

No way could she explain that Northstar would've backed off now that she'd agreed to do his bidding. Which left the troubling question of just who was trying to kill her.

"I see. Well, if it's not the NFR, then who the hell is it? Have more than one group pissed off at you, Jules? Maybe it has something to do with the people you've assassinated over the years."

If he had lashed out and struck her full in the face, she wouldn't have felt worse. She sucked in her breath and felt the blood drain from her face. "That's low, Manny." She opened the car door and got out. She needed the air, and she'd be damned if she spent another minute in the car.

Manny bolted around the car before she could stalk away. He grabbed her shoulders and forced her to look at him. "How do they know where we are?"

Was it possible for him to think any lower of her? "Do you honestly think I'm leading them to us?" she asked in disbelief.

His eyes glittered in anger. "I don't know what to think. You just said it wasn't the NFR. Yet whoever it is has the uncanny knack of finding us. They're one step ahead of us no matter where we go."

She jerked away from him. "Get in the car and leave, Manny. I don't need you. I can take care of myself. Everything I've done is to keep my family—you—safe."

"Goddamn it, I'm not going anywhere. I just want you to tell me the truth."

"The truth? I have no idea what the truth is. All I know is that this isn't the work of the NFR. Doesn't fit their M.O."

Manuel stared at Jules and bit his tongue to hold back his retort. That wasn't all that didn't fit their M.O., but he wasn't about to get into the details of her forced recruitment again. "So who is it, then?"

She shrugged and began rubbing her shoulder again. "I don't know."

"Is there something wrong with your shoulder?"

She looked up in surprise. "No, why do you ask?"

He didn't reply. "We've got to figure out how to get to D.C. without attracting any more attention. So far we've managed to make enough noise to wake the dead. I swear it's like they have a tracking device on us, but I've checked the car."

Jules went pale. Her eyes flickered, and she shuddered uncontrollably. He frowned, wondering what private hell she was enduring now.

"That's it," she whispered.

"What's it?"

"A tracking device. I'm so fucking stupid. God." She spun around and stalked back to the car, shaking her head the entire way. He followed her, perplexed by her bizarre behavior.

She wrenched open her door and began to dig furiously in her bag. With a muttered curse, she threw the bag onto the seat. She turned back to him. "Do you have a knife?"

"What? No knife in that arsenal?"

"This isn't the time for your attitude," she snarled. "Do you or do you not have a knife?"

He reached down and rolled up the cuff of his pants. Secured beside his spare pistol was a pocket knife. He pulled it out and handed it to her.

She shoved it back at him. "You're going to have to do it. I can't reach."

"What are you talking about?" He ignored the outstretched knife.

She shoved down the collar of her shirt.

"Nice tattoo," he remarked, noting the small serpent on her shoulder blade.

She flipped the knife at him, forcing him to catch it. "You're going to have to cut it open."

"You want me to do what? Are you insane? I'm sure there are safer ways of getting rid of a tattoo."

"Not the tattoo," she said through gritted teeth. "The tracking device implanted in the tattoo."

Chapter Fourteen

Jules watched the disbelief spread across Manny's face. She sighed. He was going to want a long, drawn-out explanation, and the truth of the matter was, she didn't have one. But she knew without a doubt, the haunting memories she'd been experiencing had everything to do with the way they were being found out at every turn.

"You want me to slice open your shoulder? Are you nuts?"

"That point's debatable," she replied. "But yes, you're going to have to dig out the tracking device unless you want the bad guys to keep turning up everywhere we go."

"You're crazy. No way I'm cutting you open with a damn pocket knife."

"Don't be a wuss, Manny. I've suffered a lot worse. You know it's the only option we have, so just get it over with."

"I am not slicing you open in a public parking lot," he growled.

"Then let's find a place you will. And quickly, if you don't mind. I'd rather not deal with more attempts on my life today."

He looked horrified by the notion, but she also saw the realization in his eyes that she was right. Still, his distaste was evident.

"Get in," he said shortly. Then he strode around to the driver's side.

Jules slid into the seat and looked over at him. "Should we find another hotel? We'll have to make it quick if we don't want to be ambushed."

"No. I don't want to box us in. We'll find an open area. God, I hope you're right, Jules. I don't want to be cutting you up for nothing."

"I'm right." She knew it without a doubt. She could still feel the searing pain of the knife as it sliced her back open. The fingers parting her flesh. They had planted the device then given her the tattoo to cover the scar. The bastards had always known where she was. She never had a chance. Mom and Pop never had a chance.

So as it turned out, she had in fact killed them with her carelessness.

"Why did you only now realize you were being tracked?" he asked.

She closed her eyes. She knew how damning it looked. Someone wasn't likely to forget they had a piece of metal in their back. She'd effectively blocked the events of that day from her mind until it had been time to tell Manny what had happened. "I don't expect you to believe that I didn't know until now. The important thing is for us to get rid of the device."

His lips thinned but he remained silent. She could see a slight tic in his jaw, though. He was angry. He had reason. She couldn't fault him for that.

He drove through the crowded streets, and she kept careful watch for suspicious activity around them. After several city blocks, the buildings gave way to a large, grassy park. She nodded approvingly. The area was wide open. No one would be able to sneak up on them.

After parking in a place easily departed from, he switched off the engine and turned to her. "Can we do this in the car? I'd rather not chance you attracting attention with any hollering."

She stared steadily at him. "I'd prefer to do it outside."

He studied her for a moment then apparently decided she could handle it. Wordlessly, he opened the door and got out, taking the pocket knife with him. She opened her door and stepped out, her stomach lurching at what was to come. But she wouldn't let him see her fear. She'd braved worse. She wasn't going to make an ass of herself in front of him.

Manuel watched as she slowly stood up and shut her car door. She shrugged out of her jacket and threw it over the hood. "Where should I stand?"

He glanced around their surroundings. This was absurd. He couldn't cut open her shoulder in broad daylight in a public park. Discounting the fact that he had no desire to hurt her, if they drew attention again, it was going to be damn difficult to extricate themselves.

"Jules, you're going to have to get in the car. We can't do it out here. I can leave the door open."

She didn't look thrilled by the announcement, but she nodded her understanding. He opened the back door then looked at her. "If you can just kneel down and face the door, I can shield the other side of you with my body."

She complied, her fingers gripping the inside armrest of the door as she knelt on the pavement. He pulled up her shirt and quickly looked around to make sure no one was close. She trembled as he thumbed the small tattoo. Damn. There was no way to make this painless.

"Just do it," she gritted out.

He flipped open the knife and set the point at the top of the tattoo. Not wanting to prolong her agony, he sliced down in a

127

quick motion, flaying open the skin about an inch. She flinched, and he could hear her sucking in her breath.

Using the back of her shirt, he soaked up the blood that ran down her back. Then he gently pressed the point of the blade into the wound, feeling for any obstruction. To his surprise he came across a small, round disk no larger than a hearing-aid battery. He flicked it out into his palm and pressed her shirt firmly over the wound. "I've got it."

Frowning, he stared down at the metal object. He was familiar with the technology, and as far as he knew, it wasn't something the NFR would have access to. Shelving his questions for the moment, he turned his attention back to Jules.

He helped her up, keeping a steadying hand to her back. "Are you okay?" His heart lurched when he saw the pain in her eyes.

She nodded. "Is it still bleeding?"

"Yeah. It really needs stitches, but we'll have to settle for stopping and getting some bandages somewhere. I'll need to wash it out with an antiseptic too."

She stared pointedly at his hand. "What are you going to do with that?"

"No sense tipping our hand by destroying it. Better to lead them away from us." He glanced around, his eyes lighting on a nearby bus stop.

"Get in the car and wait for me," he directed. "I'm going to go plant the device on the bus."

She got into the car, and he could see the red stain at her back growing larger. He needed to get to a drugstore fast. He sprinted across the grass as he saw the bus approaching from down the street. When the bus pulled up, he boarded and looked at the driver. Pretending to dig into his pockets for change, he grimaced. "Sorry, must have forgotten my cash." He quickly dropped the tracking device on the floor and stepped off the bus.

As it drove away, he hurried to the car. He climbed in and looked over at Jules in concern. "You okay?" She was pale and shaking. Her eyes reflected an inner turmoil that he imagined had nothing to do with the wound he'd inflicted on her.

"I'm fine. Let's get out of here."

He nudged her forward and frowned when he took in the amount of blood covering her shirt. "After I bandage you up, you need to get another shirt on."

"Manny, can we just go?"

He fired the engine and pulled away. As they drove from the park, he kept his eyes peeled for a place he could buy medical supplies. After several blocks, he spied a small drugstore and pulled over. "Wait here."

Jules watched him walk into the drugstore and marveled at how easily he trusted her. Had he forgotten how hard she'd tried to ditch him? She leaned back against the seat, not caring if she got blood all over the leather.

So much had happened in the last few days. Her life had changed irrevocably. Manny's life had changed. She wondered how much he resented her. He'd been nothing but caring, but when he found out the truth about her and what she planned... She shivered at the thought. Of all the things she'd suffered, his hatred was something she couldn't bear.

Her shoulder throbbed, slick with blood. The smell nauseated her, bringing back the memory of when they had implanted it.

Bastards.

She squeezed her eyes shut and tried to block out the hatred, the desire for revenge. It would only make her vulnerable. And careless. But after so many years of coldness, she was awash with raw feeling. She was bombarded at every angle by differing emotions. Sorrow. Regret. Loss.

Goddamn it, she would not cry again.

Manny returned with a small bag, and she ignored his scrutinizing look. As he closed the door behind him, he motioned for her to twist in the seat.

"Take your shirt off," he directed. "I bought you a T-shirt you can wear."

After a moment's hesitation, she tore off the bloodied shirt, keeping her chest to the door. Not that the sight of her boobs would send his hormones raging, but she would not feel any more vulnerable than she already did.

She flinched when his hand gently closed on her shoulder. A cool rag wiped over her wound as he worked methodically to clean it.

"Okay, this is going to hurt."

She barely had time to suck in her breath before her back lit on fire. She let out her air in a long hiss of pain as the antiseptic danced daggers on her shoulder.

His thumbs pressed into her skin as he taped a bandage over the wound. Then he thrust the shirt at her.

She hastily pulled it over her head.

"It's not the best, but it'll do."

She nodded. "Where to now?"

He sighed and started the engine then threw the BMW into reverse. He looked over his shoulder as they backed out of the parking lot and headed onto the street.

"I need to call Tony. We still need to get to D.C."

She didn't respond, and only halfway paid attention as he got on his cell phone to correspond with his partner.

Yes, they had to get to D.C. Her destiny awaited her in D.C. Her last miserable effort to try and get out of the life she had made for the last three years, and then she'd disappear and hope Manny could get on with his life.

She clenched her fingers into balls in her lap, her ragged nails digging painfully into her palms. If only she could draw Northstar out, she could put an end to everything. She'd take pleasure in killing the bastard who had heaped so much pain on her.

Manny's hand crept over hers, uncurling her tightly wound fingers. "You're drifting again, baby."

She cringed. The endearment was back. He never could stay angry at her for long. Unable to help herself, she gripped his hand, holding tightly to it like a lifeline. She hadn't even realized he had finished talking to Tony.

Composing herself the best she could, she turned her head to Manny. "What did Tony say?"

He sighed. "We drive to Beaumont, and he'll have another car lined up for us. Then we hit the road to D.C."

"Another Bondmobile?"

He halfway grinned. "If Tony lined it up, it'll have all the bells and whistles."

She leaned back in her seat. "I'm sorry, Manny. I never meant to involve you in my problems."

His hand cupped her chin, forcing her to look at him.

"I just wish you had involved me three years ago."

Chapter Fifteen

They drove down Interstate 10 as fast as Manuel dared without drawing attention from any passing state troopers. Jules slumped in her seat looking unbelievably exhausted. He could relate. Fatigue had long since set in with him. He only wanted a safe place where they both could rest, and he could take care of her.

When they arrived in Beaumont, as Tony promised, another vehicle waited for them at the rendezvous point. They ditched the Beamer for an SUV then headed north, paralleling Louisiana through Southeast Texas.

His neck ached. His back ached. Hell, he hadn't felt this bad since he was in high school when he tied one on graduation night.

Jules broke the silence. "Let me drive."

He glanced over at her. "I'm okay."

She snorted. "You look like you're about to fall over. Let me drive. I won't kill us. I promise."

He sighed and pulled off. He'd pick his battles, and frankly this wasn't one of them.

They changed seats, and he settled back, watching her from the corner of his eye. She gripped the steering wheel tightly, her gaze directed forward, but at rapid intervals she checked the rearview and side-view mirrors.

He opened his mouth, wanting to ask so many questions, but he halted before the first word left his lips. Truth be told, he didn't even want to know the answers. And he didn't want her to relive memories of her hell.

Never again, he vowed silently. She was his to protect.

"Do you want to stop for the night?" she asked, glancing over at him. "Or should we keep driving?"

"We should probably drive as long as we can," he replied. "Put as much distance between us and the baddies as possible. We can stop when we reach Tennessee. Tony will line us up a spot."

"You trust him."

It wasn't a question, but she voiced it as if surprised. But then he supposed she had learned to trust no one.

"Yes, I trust him. With my life. Our lives," he added for emphasis.

She nodded, and Manuel felt a twinge of hope that she was allowing herself to trust *him.*

"Want me to drive?"

She smiled. "No, I've only been driving an hour. Why don't you get some sleep? You can take over when we reach Arkansas."

"Okay. Wake me."

She nodded again.

Jules watched as he dozed off, his head leaning on his shoulder. She ached to reach out and touch him, burrow into his arms and sleep as well. She was nearly past her breaking point, exhaustion seeping from her every pore. But she knew

Manny needed rest. She'd gone without sleep before, sometimes for days. She could certainly do it again.

She focused her attention on the never-ending road in front of her. The towns passed in a blur, and darkness began to fall. When she reached Texarkana, she turned east on the interstate toward Little Rock.

Who was trying to kill her? She had no doubt Northstar had known her every movement, but why after she'd agreed to do the job had someone tried to kill her? No one else should even know where she was.

Beside her, Manny's cell phone pulsed and vibrated. She yanked it up and hit the button to silence it so it wouldn't wake him.

She drove on mechanically, maneuvering through traffic, counting mile markers to stay awake. When they were a few miles outside Little Rock, Manny stirred beside her and shifted up in his seat.

"You okay?" he asked, his voice still heavy with sleep.

"Yeah."

"Want me to drive?"

Instead of speaking, she pulled onto an exit and parked at a gas station. They needed to fill up anyway. She turned off the ignition and leaned forward, resting her head against the steering wheel.

Strong hands stole over her back, creeping up, massaging her neck and shoulders, careful around her wound.

"You need to sleep, baby," Manny said, his voice full of love and concern. "I'll pump the gas. You want anything from inside?"

She shook her head and opened the door to get out. The cool air did little to revive her. It wasn't as cold as in Colorado.

She walked around the front, meeting Manny as he moved toward the pump.

To her surprise, he caught her in his arms and pulled her to his chest, enfolding her completely in his embrace. He stroked her back comfortingly, taking care not to bump her bandage.

She laid her head on his chest, soaking up the moment like the desert does the rain. He kissed her on top of the head and slowly pulled away.

"Get in and get some rest," he ordered. "We'll be on the road again in a few minutes."

She slid into the seat and sighed. It was still warm from Manny's body. She curled closer to the leather, wanting to absorb his presence.

A few minutes later, Manny got behind the wheel and started the engine.

"Someone called for you while you were asleep," she said as they drove from the parking lot.

"It was probably Tony."

She shrugged. "Maybe."

He stared at her for a moment then reached for his phone.

She turned away and looked out the window, searching the sky for answers she knew she wouldn't find. Behind her, Manny spoke in low tones. She supposed Tony was giving him information on the place in Tennessee. Or giving Manny more dirt on her. As if he didn't know enough already.

She felt his touch on her back and turned around. He was off the phone.

"Get some rest. We've got another six hours before we get to the place Tony squared away for us."

She nodded and scooted down in her seat. Six hours. It was a long time and yet not nearly enough time. She wanted so much to...

It didn't matter. She closed her eyes. What she wanted she couldn't have, and there was no use dwelling on it.

Chapter Sixteen

Around two a.m., Manny pulled into the drive of a log cabin situated on a large lake. Jules was exhausted, but she hadn't slept. Her nerves were too jagged.

They stepped into the cold night air, and she inhaled sharply, hoping the bite would sharpen her senses. She followed Manny to the door, and as he had done in New Mexico, he drew his gun and pushed the door open, sticking his gun in first, then following slowly behind.

"Find the light switch," he whispered.

She fumbled along the wall until she found the switch, and light flooded the foyer.

"Stay here while I check the rest of the house."

She sighed but didn't argue. Let him play super agent. She was too damn tired to go looking for bogeymen in the closet.

A few minutes later, he returned, and he motioned her into the living room.

He looked at her, uncertainty flickering across his face. "Do you want to go straight to bed?"

She stood still, not really knowing how to respond. She was tired. More tired than she'd ever been in her life, but the idea of going to a dark room alone scared her more than she wanted to admit.

"I can build a fire if you want, and we can sit in here for a while," he offered. "I need to change your bandage as well."

Had he read her so easily? She was going to have to work on keeping her thoughts from her face. She hadn't survived the last three years by being a walking billboard.

"Sounds great," she finally said.

She walked around to the couch situated close to the large stone fireplace and settled down, tucking her legs underneath her.

He piddled around the hearth for a few minutes, gathering newspapers stacked to the side and crumpling them under the grate. Then he went outside, and she heard scraping and thumping. Seconds later he returned with an armload of wood and began arranging it in the fireplace.

Soon flames licked over the dry wood and the hearth came alive with the crackle of fire. He rummaged around in one of the bags he'd brought in and carried over a bandage and the antiseptic.

She turned around to present her back and tensed as she awaited his attentions. His fingers were gentle as he peeled off the tape. She heard the slosh of the liquid then felt fire on her shoulder as he swabbed a cloth over the cut.

She let out a long hiss and closed her eyes.

"I'm sorry."

She shook her head and remained still while he arranged another bandage over the wound. When he was finished, he pulled her back until she reclined against the sofa.

"Long day."

"Mmm hmm."

Awkward silence settled between them, and the effort for idle chitchat died. She stared into the fire, the warmth reaching out and enveloping her.

Manuel watched the protective way she held her arms around her. He doubted she even realized how vulnerable it made her look.

Her eyes flitted sideways at him several times as if she wanted to ask something but couldn't quite muster the courage. In the past, she would have never hesitated to ask him anything. Sadness crept over his shoulders, tightening his chest.

"Manny?"

"Yes, baby?"

"Did you mean what you said before? At the restaurant?"

He furrowed his brows in confusion.

Her breath hiccupped in a soft rush. "About...about wanting to marry me?"

He closed his eyes for a second. "Yeah, Jules. I meant it."

"Oh."

She looked panicked, as if she had no idea how to respond.

He reached a hand out, feathering over her cheek, feeling the smoothness of her skin. His fingers curled around her chin, his thumb swirling close to her ear.

"Is that all you can say? Oh?"

Her eyes found his, so full of pain, questions and something that looked remarkably like hope.

"I just never imagined..." Her voice trailed off, and she looked away.

Her shoulders shook silently, each twitch shooting an arrow directly into his soul.

He leaned forward and pulled her into his arms, turning her back around to face him. Her gaze found his, and there was so much vulnerability in her eyes. So much that he wanted to wipe away. He lowered his lips to her forehead.

A breathy sigh escaped her as he blazed a path to her lips.

"I wanted nothing more than for you to come home from France and spend the rest of your life with me," he said as he brought both of his hands up to cup her face.

She leaned into him, burrowing into his embrace. His hands fell away as she pressed her face into his chest. He held her as tightly as he dared, not wanting to hurt her ribs.

Her face nuzzled in his chest, then her soft mouth turned upward, finding his neck. She kissed it softly, sending a shockwave down his spine.

He slid his hand around her neck, running his fingers through her hair. She felt so right in his arms, as if she had always belonged there. He had waited so long, and now that she was here, he was having a hard time grappling with his control.

After what had happened to her, she deserved tenderness, and he'd be damned if he gave her anything but.

"Let's sleep in here," she murmured. "By the fire."

"If that's what you want." He reluctantly pulled away. "I'll get some blankets and pillows."

Jules watched him walk toward the bedroom, and she stood up from the couch, moving closer to the fire. She wasn't cold. Far from it. The heat from Manny's body had scorched her.

She wasn't afraid. She knew he would never hurt her. No, she knew just the opposite was true. She'd hurt him. But she wanted this night. Wanted it more than anything in the world.

Wanted to erase the awful events of that long-ago day when her entire world had been turned upside-down.

Manny returned carrying a bedspread and several pillows. She gestured to the floor in front of the fire. The carpet was soft, plush. They could make do with just the blanket for padding.

He knelt down and spread out the covers then arranged the pillows so their bodies would parallel the fire. He stretched out on his side and propped his elbow on the floor. Then he patted the space beside him.

She went to him without hesitation, nestling her back to his chest so she could face the fire. His hand rested on the curve of her shoulder, and he bent to kiss her neck as she had done to him earlier.

Goose bumps spread out over her arms and neck as desire warmed places of her heart long left cold.

She closed her eyes as his hand moved to her waist and over her hip. His lips followed. He was achingly gentle, each touch feather light, yet she felt each one to her core.

She rotated around until she faced him, sure uncertainty was carved on her face. With a shaking hand, she reached out to touch his cheek. He captured her fingers in his much larger hand and pressed the tips to his mouth, kissing them one by one.

"Do you have any idea how long I've dreamed of this moment?" he asked. "Holding you in my arms, knowing you were mine to love."

"Don't let me go," she whispered.

"Never."

He rolled her over, his hand going behind her head to cushion her. He held himself over her, staring down at her. "I won't hurt you, Jules. I'll never hurt you."

"I know."

And she did know.

He tugged at her shirt, loosening it from her jeans. His palm slid over her abdomen, pushing the shirt upwards, over her breasts. He bent and pressed his mouth to the bruises on her ribcage, kissing the hurt with such exquisite tenderness her throat swelled and ached with unspent emotion.

She closed her eyes as he worked the shirt over her head and tugged it free of her arms. Slow heat worked its way over her body when his fingers drifted down to her pants.

He rose up, his hand falling away from her waist. He pulled his shirt over his head and tossed it to the side. Lord, he was so big, his chest broad, showcasing muscular arms. He was every inch the warrior. The protector of the innocent.

Only she wasn't innocent.

A shadow hovered over her as the unwanted thought drifted through her mind. Manny must have sensed her dismay and lowered himself, collecting her in his arms.

Flesh met flesh. She delighted in the feel of their naked bodies melting together. He was hard to her softness, strength to her weakness. For the space of a few minutes, she felt so incredibly safe. Cherished.

She didn't want to let go of this moment. She might never have this again, and she wanted it to go on and on.

She raised her lips to meet his, fusing their mouths like molten liquid. She released all the pent-up longing, all her childlike fantasies and her womanly desires.

He returned her frantic kisses, swallowing her sighs of pleasure. His hand gripped her hip, cupping her to the hardness still trapped by his jeans. She felt the scratch of denim as her legs moved with restless abandon.

"Take them off," she whispered.

He pulled from her long enough to shimmy his jeans down and kick them away. He turned his gaze back to her, and she shivered at the intensity in his eyes.

"You're beautiful, Jules. More beautiful than ever."

She smiled half in amusement, half in self-conscious discomfort. She'd never looked worse, but she imagined he thought she looked beautiful because he hadn't seen her in so long. She understood. He had never looked more beautiful to her than in this moment. Naked next to her in front of the fire.

He began at her navel, kissing lightly, raining a trail of fire from her abdomen to her breasts. She sucked in her breath when his tongue swirled around first one nipple then the other. She closed her eyes and groaned aloud when he finally pulled one into his mouth.

An unbearable need blossomed in her stomach and spread to her groin. One only he could sate. Gone was the terror and shame of long ago. This was a man she had waited forever for.

His hand parted her thighs, and he stroked soothingly over her tender flesh. His fingers performed magic, and she began to move beneath him, wanting more.

He kissed her again, his tongue delving deep into her mouth, staking his claim.

"Are you all right?"

She didn't trust herself to speak so she nodded. His fingers pushed her hair from her forehead, tucking it behind her ears. He looked at her with such love and acceptance, she wanted to cry. How would he look at her when he learned of her betrayal?

Her breath came out in a shaky jerk.

Manny's gaze softened even more.

"Don't be afraid, baby. I'll never let anyone hurt you again."

She didn't correct his assumption. She couldn't.

He kissed her lightly, tenderly, and the aching in her heart increased tenfold.

She reached out to touch his chest, her fingertips glancing over the hard muscles and light smattering of hair. He rolled onto his back, coaxed by her hands. She followed him, eager to explore more of his body.

He groaned. "I've dreamed of you touching me."

Encouraged by his response, she followed her fingers with her lips. She inhaled deeply, letting his scent envelop her senses. His taste danced a slow waltz on her tongue, warm and comforting.

She paused for a moment when she saw the evidence of his arousal. Hard and erect, yet when she touched it, it felt satiny and smooth.

"God, Jules."

His voice came out tortured, ragged.

She smiled, enjoying her power over him. She bent to kiss him there, but he caught her shoulders.

"Don't, baby. I won't last if you do."

He pulled her up his body until her head was even with his again. Then he rotated over her, his length covering hers. He supported himself with his hands so his weight didn't crush her, but she felt every inch of him.

For a long moment he simply stared down at her, his gaze stroking over her flesh just as his hands had done just seconds ago.

"I love you."

She stared at him in shock, too overwhelmed to respond, her heart nearly bursting from her chest.

And still he stared as if willing her to accept the words. His eyes were dark with emotion. Love. She couldn't deny it. She didn't want to. He loved her.

He waited silently, allowing her time to absorb his confession, to accept that he wasn't simply going to have sex with her. Her chest tightened, painful with each breath she tried to let loose.

She lifted her hand to cup his cheek and then smoothed her thumb over the lines under his eyes, over his cheekbone and then down to his jaw. She wanted so much to tell him she loved him. Adored him. Always had. But it seemed the ultimate betrayal when she planned to turn her back on the love he offered so unconditionally.

But she could show him.

Her hands wandered down his body, over his broad shoulders and then to his chest, coming together in the hollow where she could feel the steady beat of his heart.

"Show me," she finally said. It was all she could say.

He closed his eyes and when he reopened them, they were bright with desire. Worry for her. And love. So much love that she felt it wrap around her and invade her soul.

He nudged her legs apart with his thigh and settled his heavy erection against her opening. She hooked her ankles around his waist, encouraging him, wanting him.

He closed his eyes again and the muscles in his neck strained and bulged as he began to slowly ease his way into her body. He was so exquisitely tender, so reverent that her eyelids burned with unshed tears. Didn't he know that she trusted him? That she knew he'd never hurt her?

She wrapped her arms around him, wanting him closer, wanting the security of his big body so close to hers. And she hung on, burying her face in his neck, her eyes squeezed shut against the emotion building in her heart.

"I love you," he said again, as if he knew just how much she needed to hear the words.

He slid his arms underneath her, gathering her as closely as she held him. Their bodies were meshed so tight that there was no space between them, no point of separation. They moved as one, finding their rhythm as he stroked in and out of her in long, tender thrusts.

At intervals, he paused and kissed her hair, her temple, her cheek, any part of her he could reach with his mouth. Her heart melted a little more because she knew how close he was to his release and yet he waited for her, wanting her to be with him.

And then he'd begin again, driving her mindless, bringing her ever closer to something she wasn't sure of. But she wanted it. She wanted it more than anything.

She twisted restlessly and then arched her body up, but he quieted her with a hand to her hip.

"We've got all night, baby. No hurry. Just us enjoying each other. Let me love you like you deserve to be loved."

She sighed and relaxed, willing to let him take over.

"That's it," he murmured.

He lowered his mouth to hers and kissed her. Long, hot, breathless kisses that left her panting. He ravaged her mouth and then moved down her jaw to her neck, marking her, claiming her. Telling her without words that she was his.

He moved down to kiss her breasts and when he slid from her body, she felt the loss and reached to pull him back, but again he put out a gentle hand to stop her.

"Relax. I've waited a long time to be able to see you this way. I'm going to take my time."

She sighed again and stared down as his dark head lowered to her nipples. He sucked and toyed with each one in turn and then caressed the small mounds, holding them for his eager lips.

He hadn't lied. He licked and nibbled until she was nearly crazy with desire. And when he finally lifted his head away, she thought he'd finally push back inside her again, but he moved further down her body until he was positioned between her thighs, his shoulders holding her open for him.

Tiny little shivers quaked over her skin when his mouth touched her most intimate flesh. She closed her eyes, helpless against the onslaught of such pleasure. Her fingers curled into tight balls at her sides. Her knees shook. Her legs quivered and went limp as he coaxed her higher and higher.

He kissed and sucked gently. The long swipes of his tongue made her crazy with wanting. She arched, her muscles tightening as her release built. She was so close. So very close. One more... Just one more touch...

His mouth left her and he crawled back up her body, his eyes blazing with a fierceness that made her tremble. He slid back into her in one long thrust. Their hips met and he held himself deep. Then he began to move, his pace more urgent than before. His face was tight with strain—strain she felt in every part of her body.

She wrapped herself around him, molding her body to his, holding on like she'd never let go. His mouth pressed against her ear and his ragged breaths spilled down her neck. Then she closed her eyes and let out a small cry as the world shattered and blurred around her.

He was close behind her. The moment she peaked, he let out a groan of his own and buried his face in her neck. His hips pumped against hers and then he went rigid over her, his muscles bulging underneath her fingertips.

Even as they melted into the covers beneath them, he kept himself deep inside her.

Gradually her body relaxed, the series of quakes lulling, leaving her drained, but still she held on to Manny.

His hand stroked soothingly over her hair. He murmured in her ear. Words of love and approval that she soaked in like someone starving for water.

He rolled to his side, still holding her in his arms.

She burrowed deeper into his embrace, her face nestled in the crook of his neck. For tonight she wouldn't worry about tomorrow or what she must do. Tonight she lay in the arms of a man who loved her, and whom she loved with everything she possessed.

Chapter Seventeen

Dawn crept through the windows, bathing the living room in pale light. Manuel rubbed his eyes then raised his arm to glance at his watch.

Jules lay next to him, curled trustingly against his chest. Unable to help it, he put his arm back over her and pulled her even closer. She stirred but snuggled further into his embrace and stayed asleep.

A rush of satisfaction more powerful than he'd ever experienced surged through his veins. He bent his head to nuzzle her hair, inhaling her sweet scent. He rubbed his lips over her softness, kissing her gently enough not to awaken her.

He couldn't remember ever being this happy, not in the last three years, for sure. As soon as the thought hit him, he grimaced. There was nothing to be happy about in their present circumstances.

They couldn't simply ride off into the sunset and live happily ever after. No hope of a picket fence and a normal existence. She was a *terrorist*, and he was in the CIA's premiere counter-terrorism unit. If his superiors found out about Jules, his ass was cooked and so was hers.

It was enough to make him want to take Jules and run as far as they could, away from the CIA, away from the NFR. But he wasn't a coward, and there were too many unanswered questions. With Tony's help, he hoped to get some answers.

He slipped his other arm from beneath Jules and gently eased away from her. He held his breath as she stirred once more, and let it out in relief when she didn't wake.

He needed coffee, and he needed to call Tony. He pulled on his jeans, leaving his shirt on the floor. A quick check of his pocket found the cell phone still there. A second later, the phone rang.

Manuel looked down to see it was Sanderson. Anxiety churned in his gut. Would it be another ultimatum? He briefly considered letting it ring, but if the CIA was coming after him and Jules, he at least needed to know about it.

"Boss man," Manuel said into the phone. He tried to sound unaffected, but he wasn't sure he pulled it off.

He heard a long-suffering sigh. "Manuel, what the hell have you gotten yourself into?"

Fuck. He remained silent, waiting for Sanderson to continue.

"I'd love to know why your fingerprints came across my computer courtesy of the Houston P.D."

"Just a misunderstanding," Manuel said.

"Look, it's obvious to me you're protecting your girl. Damn it, Manuel, you've put me in a hell of a predicament. I've got the higher-ups breathing down my neck wanting to know what the fuck is going on with a suspected terrorist on the loose."

Manuel closed his eyes. "I'm sorry, sir."

"You be careful, Manuel. You're officially on your own. I'll do what I can to keep the heat from you, and I'm sure Tony's doing the same, damn his computer geek hide, but there's nothing I can do if you're apprehended, you got me?"

"Thanks," Manuel said quietly. "I won't let you down. I'm just trying to figure this mess out. Things aren't as they appear."

Sanderson snorted. "That much is obvious. Watch your back, Manuel. Your girl is bringing down a lot of heat."

The line went dead. He clenched his fist around the cell phone and squashed the urge to fling it across the room.

He needed coffee in the worst way.

As he padded into the kitchen, he wondered in a brief moment of horror if there was a coffeemaker. Tony wouldn't do that to him, though. He wouldn't send him to a place that had no coffee.

After scrounging around the cabinets, he located a coffeemaker and a canister of coffee. He sniffed it cautiously, but it didn't smell stale. Soon the aroma of the heavenly brew filled the kitchen. God, he needed three cups to make up for the last few days.

He was on his second when Jules shuffled into the kitchen. He smiled when he saw she had pulled his shirt on. It hung to her knees, but on her it looked adorable.

She looked nervously at him. He set his cup down on the counter and moved toward her, enfolding her in his arms. He kissed the top of her head.

"Good morning."

"Morning," she returned, her voice muffled by his chest.

He pulled her away and stared down into her eyes. "Are you all right? How's your shoulder?"

"I'm good. Shoulder hurts, but not bad."

"Sit down." He gestured toward a nearby barstool. "I'll rustle up some breakfast for us."

She pulled the barstool up to the bar that separated the kitchen from the small dining area and sat down. She put her elbows on the hard surface and rested her chin in her palms, studying him as he puttered around the kitchen.

"When do we leave?"

Manuel placed a skillet on the stovetop and turned to look at her. "I hoped to stay here a day or two. Let things calm down before we hit the road again. It'll give Tony time to sort out this mess on his end. But I'm waiting for him to call. We'll do what he thinks is best."

A flare of alarm crossed her face. He narrowed his eyes as he took in her reaction. What was going through her mind now?

"Is that a problem?"

She shook her head. "No, I mean that is, I thought we were in a hurry to get to D.C. I don't want you out here with me...where you can get killed."

That wasn't all she was thinking. He'd bet his life on that much, but damned if he knew what. He sighed. Would he ever get to the bottom of things? Would he ever know what truly happened to her or was it destined to remain a mystery?

He cracked eggs to make an omelet and a few minutes later set a plate in front of Jules. "Eat up. You're too thin."

She smiled slightly, but dug into the omelet with her fork. "You didn't seem to mind how thin I am last night."

His body stirred to life as he remembered just how much he hadn't minded. He set his own plate on the opposite side of the bar from her and stared directly into her eyes.

"There's nothing about you I mind, but that doesn't mean I don't worry about you."

She flushed pink, her pupils flaring for a moment. With desire?

She put her fork down, her fingers still wrapped tightly around it. She didn't raise her head to look at him, and he had to strain to hear what she said.

"I would have, you know."

He cocked his head sideways. "Would have what?"

"Married you," she said in a quiet voice. "I adored you back then. Worshipped the ground you walked on."

His chest clenched, silent agony squeezing him until he struggled for breath.

"And now, Jules? How do you feel about me now?"

She uncurled her fingers from her fork and put her hand in her lap. She still refused to look at him. When she did raise her eyes to meet his, they were awash in anguish.

"Isn't it obvious? That you mean more to me than anyone else in the world? It's why I can't allow anything to happen to you. I let Mom and Pop down. I won't let *you* down. I won't let you get killed because of me."

In that moment, he knew. He knew without question that she hadn't joined the NFR of her own volition. Her agony was clearly written on her face. Which meant she had joined because of *him.* And it made him want to puke.

Maybe it was his fault. If he had just come clean before she left that he had joined the CIA, maybe she would have had faith in his ability to help her. And she wouldn't have spent the last three years in hell. She wouldn't have thought him some helpless computer geek she had to protect.

He reached across the table and took her hand in his. "We're in this together. No matter what you may think, no matter that you endured the last three years alone, the point is you will never be alone again."

Sadness crept into her beautiful blue eyes. She didn't believe him. That was fine. He would convince her.

His cell phone rang and he yanked it up. "Yeah."

"Hey, buddy. Look, I've got you and Jules on a flight out of the Henry County Airport in two hours."

Manual blinked in surprise. "We tried flying already. Don't you think it's too risky?" The idea of being trapped on an airplane for an indeterminate amount of time didn't rest easy with him. Not with whoever was chasing him and Jules out there. Sure, they'd gotten rid of the tracking device, but he didn't think the baddies were going to give up that easily.

"It's a small strip, mostly used for private planes. You guys need to get here as soon as possible, and this is the best I can come up with. The alternative is for you to be on the highways for the next few days, and that's too much exposure."

"You're right," Manuel conceded. "We'll be on it."

"See you soon, then."

Manuel looked up at Jules. "We leave in two hours."

Her expression was indecipherable, but he could swear, her body language was screaming relief. Why was she so gung ho to get to D.C.?

"I'll get our stuff," she said as she slid off the barstool.

He wanted to reach out and touch her again. Feel her in his arms. Last night hadn't been nearly enough. It would never be enough and would never make up for the time they'd lost.

He looked down at his plate and shoved it away. He'd lost his appetite. He didn't know what would happen when they reached D.C. It wasn't as if he could introduce her to his coworkers. *Hey, here's the woman I love, and by the way she's a member of the terrorist group we've been trying to infiltrate for the last few years.*

His head throbbed, and he rubbed his palm over his mouth. Tony sure as hell better have some answers by the time they got to D.C. If not, this was going to be one giant cluster fuck.

The brisk morning air rushed through her nostrils as they stepped from the cabin. Jules inhaled deeply, enjoying the coolness on her face. Behind her, Manny locked the door then joined her beside the SUV.

The gravel crunched under her tennis shoes as she walked around to the back so they could stow their bags in the rear of the vehicle. When she tried the door, she found it locked.

She stuck her head around the back and called out to Manny. "You got the keys?"

Instead of tossing them to her outstretched hand, he walked back and inserted the key into the lock. He raised the door then turned to take her bag from her.

As he twisted back around, Jules heard a slight zinging. Then the back seat of the SUV shuddered. Manny emitted a curse of pain. She knew immediately what it was.

A sniper.

Chapter Eighteen

Jules threw herself over Manny, knocking him to the ground. Simultaneously, she reached for the Glock in his shoulder harness. Another bullet whined by and struck the ground over her arm.

"Goddamn it, Jules, get off me!" Manny threw her behind him and rolled over on his side. "Give me the gun!"

She ignored him. Ignored everything but the one thought most pressing in her mind. She wouldn't let him die. If the bastards wanted her, then by God, they'd have to come and get her.

She dove over Manny and hit the gravel drive with a roll. She scrambled to her feet, hearing Manny curse a blue streak behind her. She raised the Glock and pointed it in the direction the sniper's bullet had come from and ran a sideways line. Away from Manny.

Where was the cowardly bastard? She ran as fast as she could, knowing if she paused even for a minute, the sniper would be able to get a bead on her more easily. She dodged behind trees, all the while searching for any sign of movement from the direction of the gunfire.

The roar of an engine sounded behind her, and she glanced back to see the SUV barreling toward her. Manny drove like a madman to catch up to her. When he drew alongside her, she yanked the door open, not wanting to go around to the other side where the sniper would have a clear shot. She dove into the back seat, and Manny roared off, the SUV careening back onto the gravel drive and toward the main road.

"That was the most stupid, dumbass stunt you've pulled yet," he yelled. "What the hell did you think you were doing?"

She ignored his ranting, her eyes focused on his arm. His blood. Her heart lurched and sped up. Oh my God, he'd been shot.

"Manny, pull over."

He threw her a what-the-hell look over his shoulder and continued at breakneck speed down the highway.

"Manny, you've been shot!"

"No shit, Sherlock."

She clambered over the seat, landing in a heap on the passenger side. She scrambled to right herself, putting legs down and head up as she untangled her body from its awkward position.

His sleeve was tattered where the bullet had taken a swipe. She yanked it downward, tearing the material so she could expose the wound.

Her heart catapulted a few times when she saw it was only a graze. She pressed her lips to his shoulder just above the wound and closed her eyes in relief.

"I'm all right, Jules," he muttered. "Which is more than I'll be able to say for you when I stop this bloody car and turn you over my knee."

Oh God, she didn't care how angry he was. He was alive. Relatively unscathed. He could be mad at her for the rest of his life just as long as he *had* a rest of his life.

She crawled over the seat again and leaned into the back where their bags were. She dug around until she found a T-shirt then shimmied her way to the front seat.

"Got your knife?" she asked.

He sighed. He gripped the steering wheel with his injured arm and dug into his pocket with his left hand.

"It's just a scratch."

She flipped open the knife, not responding to his protest. She cut the T-shirt into long strips then tossed the knife onto the floorboard.

With one of the strips, she wiped gently at the blood and inspected the two-inch crease that marred the skin halfway between his elbow and his shoulder.

"It really needs stitches."

He snorted as he checked his mirrors.

"Did anyone follow us?"

He shook his head. "Nothing suspicious yet. It's several more miles to the airport."

His grunted when she tied one of the strips around his arm and tugged on the ends to make sure it was tight.

"Get my phone," he said. "I'm going to call Tony and tell him to have that damn pilot in the plane and ready to go when we get there. I don't want to be a sitting duck at some podunk airstrip."

She handed him the phone and sat back in her seat. As her adrenaline rush wore off, she began to shake. The more she tried to stop, the more she quivered.

Manny could have been killed.

She wanted to call Northstar and ask him what the hell he was trying to pull. He wanted her to complete a mission and yet he had people taking shots at her. The bastard was holding

Manny over her head. He had to know if Manny was killed, she'd never agree to anything he asked.

Unless it had all been a warning. A clear message to her that Northstar could find her no matter where she went, even without the tracking device. He was watching her, and if she tried to renege on her agreement, Manny would die.

She closed her eyes and tried to control the mad shaking.

"Damn it, Jules, I said I was all right," Manny said in exasperation.

She opened her eyes and looked at him, sure her heart was hanging on her sleeve, dangling by a thread.

"Don't you see, Manny? Don't you see why you can't be around me? Do you have any idea what I'd do if you were killed?"

He swore crudely. "I swear, Jules, if you don't stop being so fucking pig-headed, I'm going to tan your ass. I'm a big boy. I can take care of myself. I've been shot at, nearly blown up, had my brains scrambled more times than I can count. This isn't anything new and nothing I can't handle. If you put yourself in the kind of danger you just put yourself in back there one more time, you aren't going to have to worry about the NFR, because I'm going to make them look like a group of preschoolers. Are we clear on that?"

She laughed. She couldn't help herself. And it only served to piss him off further. His scowl deepened.

Her laughter gave way to the rise of hysteria, and suddenly she found herself unable to stop. Tears gathered in the corners of her eyes, and still she laughed harder, a desperate edge to the sound.

Manny sighed, extended his injured arm across the seat and curled his hand over hers. "I'm okay."

His voice lost the harsh anger, and it made her shake all the more. He withdrew his hand and moved it over her shoulder, rubbing up and down her back in a soothing motion.

Manuel gripped the steering wheel with his left hand until his knuckles whitened. How the hell had they been found this time? But it was clear Jules had pissed off the wrong people, and they weren't going to just let her go. And he couldn't offer her the help or the protection of the CIA. She was a terrorist, for Christ's sake. Unwilling or not, Uncle Sam wouldn't care. Capturing a member of the NFR would be a huge coup.

She made a small sound beside him, and he pulled her against his side, wincing when his arm protested. She huddled against him, and he vowed that no matter what it took, he was going to protect her.

"How much further?"

"We're in town now. Tony said it was only about five minutes from Paris."

She nodded against him and relaxed. He continued to stroke her hair as he navigated through traffic, ignoring the pain in his arm.

Several minutes later, they pulled onto a dusty county road and drove up to a hangar that resembled a metal barn. A man hopped out of a small jet and waved his arms in the air.

"You Manuel Ramirez?" he shouted over the drone of the engine.

Manuel nodded, and held out a hand to help Jules from the SUV. "I'll get our bags, you get on the plane."

She shook her head. "I'll get the bags. You're hurt."

He growled in frustration. "Get your ass on the plane, Jules. I'll get our stuff."

She set her lips firmly together, but must have realized they were open targets standing next to the SUV, so she jogged over to the plane. The pilot opened the door and helped her up.

Manuel reached into the back and collected the two bags then hurried over to the plane. He climbed in beside Jules, and the pilot taxied down the paved runway.

He breathed a sigh of relief when the plane took to the air, and he relaxed in the seat. "Are you hurting?" Jules asked.

He shifted so he turned in her direction. "Not nearly as much as I'd be hurting if you'd gotten yourself shot."

Anger flashed in her eyes. "Then why can't you see that I feel the same way about you?"

This was a dead-end argument. "I should have been there to protect you the last three years. That's not something I'm likely to ever forget. You've gone it alone for as long as you're ever going to. From now on, no one and nothing is going to hurt you without going through me first."

She made a sound of distress, but he put a finger over her lips before she could voice her objections.

He glanced toward the cockpit then back at Jules. "Let's not waste our time arguing," he murmured, leaning in to press his lips to hers.

She melted into his kiss like heated honey. Her small hands crept up his chest and around his neck. He loved the feel of her so close. Finally in his arms where she belonged.

He pulled her closer, resting his chin on top of her head. He loved her. Had loved her for so long. He couldn't remember *not* loving her.

Fear crawled a slow trail down his spine. What if he couldn't keep her safe? Now that they were approaching Washington, she was in more danger than ever. He couldn't simply hand her over to his superiors, and he wouldn't allow the terrorist bastards to take her out.

For the first time, he gave serious thought to skipping the country altogether. Take Jules to some remote island and not look back. But that didn't sit well with him either. He wasn't a traitor.

He shook his head, determined not to let doubt creep into his mind. He and Tony would figure something out. They had to.

Jules snuggled deeper into the hollow of his neck, and he kissed her silky hair.

"Did I hurt you last night?" They hadn't had any time to sort through what had happened between them. He'd been worried sick he would go too fast or frighten her, given her past rape.

She stilled against him, then she pulled away.

"No. You were wonderful."

He nudged her chin upward with the tip of his finger. "I love you, baby. Remember that. From now on, it's us. Not you. Not anymore."

For a long time she simply stared at him. Silent. Her gaze stroking over his face. Then she raised her hand to feather her fingers along his cheekbone.

"I love you too," she said in a solemn voice.

Triumph blazed a trail through his chest. He pulled her against his side, cupping her head to his shoulder. She loved him. He'd find a way for them to be together. One that didn't entail him turning her over to the government.

Chapter Nineteen

They landed on a small private airstrip in Virginia that afternoon. Jules collected her duffle bag and followed Manny off the plane toward a waiting SUV. She needed to talk to Northstar. Needed to find out what the hell was going on and why he was taking potshots at her and Manny. When Manny wasn't looking, she dug the phone out of the bag and shoved it into her pocket.

"Can you stop at a gas station so I can use the bathroom?" she asked as she slid in beside Manny.

It wasn't a lie. She was about to pop, but she'd use the opportunity to talk to Northstar out of Manny's earshot.

"I'd prefer to wait until we reach the apartment Tony has for us, but if you can't wait, I'll stop at the first one I see," he said.

"Thanks. It's about to become an emergency situation."

He chuckled and reached across the console, twining his fingers with hers.

Such a small gesture, yet it spoke volumes.

From now on, it's us. Not you. Not anymore.

God, how she wished it could be true. She *wanted* it to be true.

She looked up as they slowed and pulled into the parking lot of a gas station. She smiled gratefully at Manny.

"I'll be right back."

He nodded and turned his attention out his window.

She climbed out of the SUV and hurried inside. Manny wouldn't wait long, so she had to make it quick. As soon as she was inside the bathroom, she locked the door and pulled the phone out of her pocket.

With shaking hands, she punched in the number she hadn't called in over a year. Shuttled through endless connections, making a trace impossible, the call took several seconds to complete.

She took a deep breath and put the phone to her ear. She didn't have to wait long. On the third ring, the bastard's voice filtered through the receiver.

"You don't follow directions very well. I told you to check your e-mail. Nothing about phone communications."

She ignored his reprimand. "What's your game, you bastard? Why are you trying to kill me?"

An uncharacteristic pause swelled on his end. "If I wanted you dead, you would be in the morgue. Quit wasting my time and finish your assignment."

"If you hurt him, I will hunt your ass down," she said in chilling tones. "Lay off the snipers, Northstar. I don't know what your latest sick game is. I've said I would do the assignment, but I can't do it if I'm dead."

Another long pause on his end. If she didn't know better, she'd swear he was genuinely caught off-guard.

"Do the job, Magalie, or your boyfriend is going home in a body bag."

He hung up before she could respond. She swore viciously and shoved her phone back into her pocket. What the hell was going on? Was he trying to imply he wasn't behind the shootings? And if he wasn't, who was?

The pulse in her temple thudded painfully, a vile ache spreading to the back of her neck.

She relieved herself then hurried out of the bathroom. When she slid into the SUV, Manny looked questioningly at her.

"Everything okay?"

She nodded and forced a smile.

Manuel started the engine and drove back onto the highway. As he turned toward D.C., he pulled his cell phone out to call Tony.

"Hey man, you landed?"

"Yeah," Manuel said. "Wanted to get the location of the place you set up for me and Jules to stay."

He glanced over at Jules, but she was staring out the window. She looked tense, but he supposed she was afraid. He shouldered his phone and reached out to her with his free hand, wanting to offer reassurance.

She smiled weakly at him and squeezed his hand in return.

Keeping a careful eye on the side-view mirrors, he listened while Tony gave him directions.

"Manuel, there's something else," Tony said as he finished the instructions. A hint of excitement colored his voice.

"Talk to me," Manuel said.

"I took the liberty of doing a little recon on my own. I may have found someone sympathetic to our cause. I think he could help Jules."

Manuel straightened in his seat. "Tell me."

"Senator Denison. Word is he's on a short list to be the new Director of Homeland Security. He's very interested in cracking the NFR. It would be a huge coup for him since the CIA has never been able to get inside the organization. He wants to meet you and Jules. He's amenable to an exchange. If Jules will give him information, he may be willing to overlook her participation in the group."

Manuel's heart began to thump harder. It was too good to be true. If he could get Jules off the hook, they would have a shot at a normal life. Together.

"Do you think Jules would turn informant?" Tony continued. "In light of her history with them, I can't believe she'd feel any loyalty to the group. If what she said about her recruitment is true."

Tony left the question dangling in the air. And that was the crux of the matter. But Manuel believed her story. Her horror had been too real as she had recounted the events of that fateful day three years ago.

"I'll talk to her," Manuel said. "Set up a meeting. Just him and me. I want to hear what he has to say before I expose Jules to any potential danger."

Beside him Jules twisted in her seat, her full attention on him. He shouldered the phone again and put his hand out soothingly.

"Will do," Tony said. "He was very anxious for the meeting to take place. I'll get back to you as soon as I've set it up."

Manuel dropped the phone onto the seat.

"What was that all about?" Jules asked.

"We may have a way to get you out of this mess."

She looked startled. "I don't understand."

"Senator Denison is interested in an exchange. If you give him information about the NFR, he's willing to overlook your past transgressions."

Her mouth rounded in shock. Consternation flared in her eyes, not relief. He frowned as he took stock of her reaction.

"This is good news, Jules."

"Yeah. Of course it is," she muttered.

"I won't let you meet with him until I'm sure he's on the up-and-up," he said, hoping to reassure her.

She nodded and looked out the window.

He shook his head, perplexed by her response. Maybe she was afraid or maybe she didn't want to get her hopes up. Whatever the reason behind her less-than-enthusiastic demeanor, he aimed to change it.

"Where are we staying?" she asked.

"A townhouse outside Bethesda. We should be there in a few minutes. We'll spend the night, and hopefully tomorrow Tony will have arranged for me to meet the senator. If not, we'll lay low until he does."

She nodded and leaned back in her seat. She ran a hand through her short hair and massaged the back of her head with her fingers.

"I'm ready for a bath." She laughed self-consciously as she twirled the ends of her hair around her fingers.

He relaxed. A normal evening would be good for them. Tony had assured him he had the townhouse under guard, and that no one would get past his security measures.

He reached over and curled his hand around the nape of her neck and squeezed gently.

Chapter Twenty

Manny pulled into a one-car garage under a two-story townhouse and cut the ignition. He glanced over at Jules and cracked a half smile. "Home sweet home."

Jules eased out of her seat and reached for her bag. Manny got out and came up behind her to cup a hand around her elbow. She let him lead her toward the entrance to the townhouse. He reached in front of her and shoved the door open.

She stepped in and stood while he flipped the light switch. The hallway opened to the kitchen, and she turned the lights on there too. Beyond the kitchen, there was a step down into the living room.

Manny walked around her and went through the house, turning on a few lamps so that a soft glow lit the interior. He motioned toward the stairs. "Want to see the upstairs? We can put our bags in the bedroom."

She followed him up the carpeted stairs. There were three doors—one on either side and one straight ahead. She stuck her head in the one straight ahead first. It was a small bathroom with a shower, commode and a pedestal sink.

She backed out and opened the door on the left side of the stairs. It was a small bedroom, obviously not the master. Manny opened the door to the right and motioned her in.

Inside was a king-sized bed, a chest of drawers and a dresser. Another door beckoned from the far side of the room, and when she walked into it, she saw it was the master bath. She gave an exclamation of pleasure when she saw the garden tub. A shower stood on the right of the tub, and catty-corner to the tub was a countertop with two sinks.

"Go put your things up," Manny directed. "I'll draw you a bath."

She smiled. She couldn't help but be warmed by his desire to take care of her. She went back into the bedroom and flopped her bag on the bed. Behind her, she heard the splash of water as Manny began filling the tub.

The bed looked inviting, so she sank down, pressing her hands into the soft comforter. She closed her eyes and lay back, letting her head fall back. It felt as though she were cushioned in the clouds. Such luxuries were as alien to her as a normal existence. And yet, here she was with Manny, seeming positively domestic.

She nearly laughed aloud at the absurdity of the facade. They could play house for a day or two, but in the end, the truth would rear its ugly head. And the worst part was how much she enjoyed the idea of setting up house with Manny.

A warm hand traveled up her leg, slid under her shirt and stroked her belly. She opened her eyes to see Manny staring down at her.

She started to get up so she could head into the bathroom, but he stopped her with his hand. He pulled her to stand beside him.

"Let me," he said huskily.

A full-body shiver skated up her spine as his fingers tugged at her shirt. He pulled it over her head then let his fingers slide down her waist to her pants. He leaned in and nuzzled her neck as his fingers hooked into her waistband. Slowly, he eased the pants down her legs until she stood in only her underwear. With extreme care, he removed the bandage from her shoulder and feathered a finger over the small wound.

She trembled beside him, nervous, breathless, aching, wanting. When his hand slipped beneath the lacy scrap of her panties, she leaned toward him. He smoothed his palm over her buttocks as the underwear fell to the floor.

"Come here, baby," he whispered, pulling her close to him.

Her bare flesh met his hard chest, and she wrapped her arms around his broad shoulders. She found herself swung upwards as he lifted her effortlessly.

"Manny, your arm!" she protested.

He ignored her and carried her into the bathroom. She gasped in surprise at what she saw. Manny had lit several candles and placed them around the tub, which was filled to the brim with foamy suds.

"The bathroom was well stocked," he murmured.

"I see that. It's beautiful, Manny. Thank you."

She smiled up at him as he knelt forward to ease her into the tub. As the warm water licked over her body, she moaned.

"Oh my God, this is heaven."

"No, I'm in heaven," he corrected. "Come here." He turned her so her back was to him, and he knelt on the floor beside the tub.

He dipped a large plastic cup into the water. "Lean back."

She cocked her head back and he poured the water over her hair. He rinsed a few more times, then he reached for a bottle of shampoo sitting on the side of the tub.

A few seconds later, his hands dug into her hair as he began massaging the shampoo over her scalp.

170

She moaned in absolute ecstasy. Waves of pleasure radiated through her body as he soaped her hair. He took his time, lavishing attention on every inch of her head. He hadn't forgotten how very much she loved to have her hair messed with.

Her muscles had as much tone as a jellyfish. She lay limply against the side of the tub, water lapping at her neck. In a few more minutes, she'd be comatose.

"Lean forward," he whispered. "I'll wash your back. I need to clean your wound."

She obeyed and he began to carefully wash the still-tender area of her shoulder. Shampoo dripped from her hair and slid down her back as he massaged his way down her spine.

Again he dipped the cup into the water. She leaned her head back to keep the soap out of her eyes as he meticulously rinsed every strand.

When he was finished, he stood up beside the tub. "Wait right here. I'll get a towel."

He returned with a large towel slung over one arm. He reached his other arm down to help her out of the tub. She stood, water running down her skin, and stepped onto the bathroom floor.

He opened the towel and wrapped it around her, rubbing it over her body. When he was done, he secured the towel around her, tucking one end so it stayed up. Then he lifted her once more in his arms and walked into the bedroom.

He set her down on the bed, letting her legs hang over the side. With slow, gentle hands, he carefully unwrapped the towel. She felt him tense when his gaze swept over her nudity.

"Lean back and I'll dry your hair," he murmured. "Then I'll get something to bandage you up."

She closed her eyes as he massaged the towel through her hair. As his motion slowed, she felt his lips slide over her neck. Chill bumps raced down her arms, and a warm tingle began a slow boil in her stomach.

After a moment, he left her and returned a second later to secure a small dressing over her wound. Then she felt his lips press against the flesh just above the cut in a gentle kiss.

"I want to make love to you again."

She let out a soft moan.

He let his hands slide over her arms down her waist to her hips. Then he circled around to her belly and let his fingers glide up to her breasts. He cupped them in his hands, rubbing his thumbs over the points.

He rolled the soft peaks between his fingers as he began to nibble at the curve of her neck. She let her head fall to her shoulder, giving him better access.

She protested softly when he drew away and let his hands drop. He stood beside the bed and pulled his shirt over his head then unbuttoned his jeans.

His erection sprang free just inches from her face. She reached out, wanting to touch him. Her fingers trailed over the velvety skin, soft and yet so very hard.

What would it taste like? She wanted to find out, wanted to give back the incredible pleasure he'd given her. With a nervous sigh, she grasped him and guided him into her mouth.

Manny moaned. "You're killing me, baby."

His hand tangled in her hair, holding her head as he moved in and out of her mouth. She delighted in the power she felt racing through her veins. For the first time in a long while, she felt beautiful, womanly, desirable. And *worthy.*

Slowly, he pulled away. He bent to capture her lips then he pushed her down on the bed. "I've dreamed of this. I've wanted this for so long."

She touched his face, danced her fingertips over his firm jaw. "Oh yes," she whispered. "Love me."

His big body covered hers, and his hand slipped underneath her buttocks. Every inch of her skin was pressed to him. There was no part of her that didn't feel him to her bones.

Their lips mingled, pressed, parted. Her breath came in ragged spurts. His tongue swirled around hers. He sucked her bottom lip between his teeth and nipped playfully.

Her legs parted when his hand slipped around her waist and delved between her thighs. He knew every place to touch. He knew just how to make her fly apart.

He pressed one finger, then two into her wetness. She arched her back, pressure building low in her pelvis. "I want you inside me," she panted. "Now."

He chuckled low then emitted a growl. "I want to be there too, baby."

She reached between them and grasped him in her hand. He felt larger, harder than before. She couldn't wait any longer.

"Please, Manny. I need you."

Her words seemed to push him over the edge. He shifted her legs wider apart then surged into her, filling her in one fluid motion.

She closed her eyes at the sheer pleasure surging through her. She felt whole in his arms. Safe, cherished and protected.

She locked her legs around his waist then wrapped her arms around his neck, pulling him down, fusing her lips to his once more.

"Do." He kissed her then pulled away. "You." He smooched softly again in between words. "Have. Any. Idea. How beautiful you are?"

"You talk too much."

He laughed and rocked forward again, setting a slow, lazy pace. "You're magnificent."

Tension spread through her stomach and built into a raging inferno. She urged him faster with her legs. He rose up as his pace increased. Her hands splayed over his broad chest, running over the dips and ridges of his muscles.

"Come with me, baby," he said hoarsely.

Every muscle in her body tensed. Her body arced, tightened, and she held onto him for dear life. "Oh God, Manny."

"I have you."

She cried out as the world exploded around her. Molten pleasure rippled through her body as she bucked against him.

"That's it, Jules. God, you're beautiful."

She opened her eyes as Manny threw his head back and thrust one last time. He shook and trembled between her thighs, and she tightened her legs around his waist.

He fell forward, using his elbows to prevent his weight from crushing her. He rested his forehead on hers and lightly kissed her lips. "I love you."

She wrapped her arms tightly around him, holding him as closely as she could. If only this moment could last forever. She closed her eyes and burrowed her face into his neck.

He shifted and rolled to his side, carrying her with him so their positions were maintained. "You feel so damn good in my arms."

Not nearly as good as she felt being there.

He stroked her hair and rubbed a hand up and down her back. Then he rested his cheek on top of her head. "Sleep, baby. In one more day, we'll have all the time in the world."

Chapter Twenty-One

Manuel woke to the sound of his cell phone ringing. He pried his eyes open, and the first thing he saw were blonde wisps of hair resting over his nose.

He smiled and nuzzled his face deeper into Jules's hair. The phone went silent then immediately began ringing again.

Damn it.

He reached behind him with his left arm, careful not to move the arm Jules's head rested on. He groped for a moment until his fingers touched the phone lying on the nightstand.

"This better be good," he muttered into the phone.

"Get your ass out of bed," Tony said. "I've set up a meeting with Senator Denison in an hour. It's the only time I could schedule you in. He's got a pretty busy itinerary for the next several days."

"Shit. Where?"

"His office in the Senate Building. His aide will be expecting you."

"All right, I'll be there." He looked down at Jules and then spoke quieter into the phone. "I assume you have the townhouse closely guarded."

"Yeah, I have two FBI agents on the job." He paused for a moment to chuckle. "You know the feds, they're always up for something that would be at cross-purposes with the CIA. Your girl should be fine on her own for a while. Unless you're concerned she'll bolt?"

Tony left the question dangling, and Manuel felt a brief moment of indecision. He didn't want to expose Jules to the senator until he knew for certain it was safe, but neither did he want to leave her alone in the townhouse.

He'd have to trust her. He *did* trust her.

"No, she'll stay," he said. "Just make sure no one takes an interest in this place."

"No problem," Tony said. "Good luck with the senator."

Manuel replaced the phone on the nightstand then slowly turned over to put his arm back around Jules. She stirred in his arms and snuggled deeper into his chest.

Damn, she felt good. This was so right, waking up with her in his arms. If the meeting with the senator went as he hoped, they'd have a shot at a normal life together. And they could put the last three years behind them.

"Jules," he whispered close to her ear.

She stirred again. "Mmmm?"

"I have to go."

She pulled slightly away and looked up at him with sleepy eyes. "Go?"

"To see the senator. Tony just called. I meet with him in an hour."

"So soon?"

He nodded. "The sooner the better. We need to get you on the right side of the law so you can be protected."

He curled his finger around the ends of her hair then tugged her toward him. He nibbled at her jaw and worked his way to her lips before giving her a long, slow kiss.

"I want many more mornings like this. And the only way we're going to get them is if I go meet with the senator and see what he has to say."

She nodded and burrowed deeper under the covers.

Reluctantly, he slid out of bed and walked naked to the bathroom.

"Am I staying here?" she called.

He turned back. "Yes. There are agents watching the townhouse. You should be safe. But just in case, keep your gun close by."

She stared at him as if she didn't quite believe what she'd heard. "You're trusting me to stay here alone?"

He cocked his head sideways. "Is there any reason I shouldn't?"

She frowned and shook her head.

He smiled at her. "I'm going to take a shower now. Go back to sleep if you want."

A few minutes later, Manuel walked out of the bathroom and glanced over to see Jules asleep again. He stood staring at her for a long moment then quietly left the bedroom. So much rode on today's meeting. He just hoped like hell the senator was as receptive as Tony had suggested.

At the sound of the door closing, Jules cracked one eye and carefully surveyed the room. Manny had left. She waited for several minutes, listening for any sign he was still downstairs. When she didn't hear anything, she crawled out of bed and went to the window overlooking the street below.

She was just in time to see the SUV she and Manny had driven to Bethesda heading down the street. She whirled away from the window and sprang into action.

Her bag lay on the floor in the corner, and she fumbled through it until she found her phone. She'd spent a lot of time wondering how she would be able to check her e-mail and get Northstar's orders without Manny knowing, and now he'd made it very easy for her. Too easy.

He trusts you.

She closed her eyes. No, she wouldn't dwell on that. She spent a moment composing herself, mentally tuning out all the emotion, the pain and the anguish associated with what she had to do.

She hated that Manny went to the senator in hopes of a miracle fix and that he harbored hopes of a fairytale ending for the two of them. The CIA would never let that happen. They had Manny in their grip just like they had her. No matter what the senator might agree to, Manny would expect to settle down somewhere with a picket fence and a nice boring life, when in fact the only chance they'd ever have would be if they ran far and ran fast.

What she had to do was carry out her mission and then disappear. Let Manny continue to operate under the guise that he worked for the good guys. That ignorance would keep him alive.

She could live with more blood on her hands. She would trade her soul for his life.

When she reopened her eyes, she felt calm. She felt like the killer she'd become.

She turned the phone on and pushed the buttons to access her secure e-mail. Sure enough, one message sat in her inbox.

She read over the message, taking in the location and date of the hit. Two days. It didn't give her much time to prepare. She arched her eyebrow when she read the locale. Ronald Reagan International Trade Center. Eight a.m. A political breakfast, no doubt. But then most of her hits were political in nature.

No I.D. on the target yet. She frowned. Why the secrecy? In the past, she'd had all the information upfront. Instead she was told the target would be provided to her the morning of the assassination.

The message went on to give details on the credentials she would be provided in order to enter the building. She let out a deep breath. This one would be risky. Lots of security. That it was in the middle of D.C. didn't help.

But she hadn't spent the last three years of her life making stupid mistakes. She was good. She'd been trained well. She'd succeed, and then she'd walk away from this life forever, and in the process leave behind the man she loved.

Her eye twitched, threatening to put a crack in her metal facade. She steeled herself and shoved the dangerous thoughts aside. Manny would be safe. That was all that mattered.

She reread the message, making sure she didn't miss anything. Then her mind began to work, methodically mulling over her plan of action.

She would need to leave early and without detection. Stealth was her specialty.

Two days. Two more days with Manny before she walked down a path of no return. She was going to make the most of every minute.

"The senator will see you now."

Manuel looked up to see a middle-aged woman in a business skirt and jacket smiling at him from the door of the senator's office.

"Thank you," he said as he rose.

She gestured him inside then closed the door behind him.

Manuel walked further into the plush office as a man rose from behind a highly polished mahogany desk.

"Manuel Ramirez? I'm Senator Denison." The senator rounded the front of the desk and stuck out a hand.

Manuel gripped it and shook. "Thank you for seeing me on such short notice, sir."

"Not at all. I was very intrigued by your situation. I'm hoping we can help each other." The senator gestured to a chair. "Have a seat. Would you like a drink? Coffee? Tea?"

Manuel shook his head. "Nothing for me, thank you."

The senator walked around to his chair and sat down. He leaned back and studied Manuel for a moment. Manuel took the opportunity to return the scrutiny.

Senator Denison was distinguished-looking, but then what senator wasn't? He imagined it was a look very practiced, accomplished with money and the right clothing. Though the senator was probably close to sixty, not a gray hair dotted his head. On a brief note of amusement, Manuel wondered if it was good genes or the work of a good hairdresser. He'd bet money on the latter.

Having worked for the agency for several years, he'd developed a healthy distrust of politicians. Too many differing agendas, and too much changed every time a new president came into office. But if this one could help Jules, Manuel would revise his opinion.

"So what can I do for you?" the senator asked finally.

Manuel arched a brow. "It's my understanding that there is something I can do for you, senator."

Senator Denison's expression relaxed and he laughed. "I like you, son. Tell you what. I'll lay my cards on the table. Then you can lay yours."

Manuel nodded.

The senator leaned forward, resting his arms on the desk. "I want to crack the NFR. Your partner told me you had a certain relationship with one of its members."

"I might," Manuel replied.

"He also mentioned that you might be interested in a trade. Information for immunity."

Manuel nodded. "Complete immunity. She walks away, or we don't give you anything."

"And what exactly can she give me?"

"Names, hits, contacts. I think you'll be very interested in her story, senator, but I won't expose her unless I have your *written* guarantee that nothing happens to her."

The senator leaned back in his chair and put his hands behind his neck. "What exactly is your relationship with this woman? I gather this goes deeper than a CIA agent offering a lead on a group the agency has tried to infiltrate for the last ten years."

Manuel worked to keep his expression neutral. "She's a victim, that's all." He wouldn't give the senator more leverage by letting him know how much Jules meant to him.

The senator nodded. "Very well. I'll send over the necessary documents by courier. I trust this will remain strictly confidential. My appointment has yet to be confirmed, and it wouldn't do for the media to find out I'm offering immunity to a terrorist."

"Of course. We have nothing to gain by going public."

Senator Denison rose. "I'd like to meet her as soon as possible." He rifled through his appointment book for a moment. "I have a speaking engagement day after tomorrow. It's early, so I could meet you, say, that afternoon?"

"Here?" Manuel asked.

"No, not here. I'll let you know. We'll have to pick a better location."

Manuel nodded. "Thank you, sir."

"If she can give me everything you say, I'll have you to thank." He reached out to shake Manuel's hand again. "Until our meeting, then."

Manuel shook his hand then turned to leave. He didn't allow himself even a breath of relief until after he had left the Senate Building. Then when the cold air blew over him, he closed his eyes and let out a long sigh. Two more days. Then she'd be his, and no one could touch her.

Chapter Twenty-Two

Jules tensed when she heard the rattle of the doorknob. She willed herself to relax, then she pasted on a bright smile just in time to greet Manny as he walked into the kitchen.

"Hello, gorgeous," he said as he enfolded her in his big arms.

She melted into his embrace and turned her mouth up to receive his kiss. "How did the meeting go?" She promptly stifled a giggle at the absurdity of the question. She sounded like Holly Homemaker asking her man how a business meeting went at the end of a day at work.

Manny guided her into the living room and sat her down on the couch beside him.

"It went well. The senator is willing to help us in return for your full cooperation."

"So he wants me to tell him everything I've seen and done for the last three years." She had never told another soul all the things she had done. Not even Manny. She could barely admit them to herself, let alone a complete stranger.

"Yes. If you give him everything you know, he'll give us his guarantee that you won't be punished for your involvement."

"And you believe him?"

"Yes."

She nibbled on her bottom lip as she studied the hope burning in Manny's eyes. She'd give anything to be able to lay everything out for the senator, trust him with her life. The problem was, she didn't trust him with *Manny's* life. And he was the one in danger.

"When does he want to meet with me?"

"Day after tomorrow. In the afternoon."

She breathed an inward sigh of relief. By then she would be long gone. She wouldn't have to face that particular obstacle.

"Let's make lunch," she suggested, standing up beside the couch.

Manny followed her into the kitchen. "You sit. I'll cook."

So she sat at the bar and watched while he clanked around in the cabinets. After surveying the contents of the refrigerator, he stuck his head out and looked back at her. "How's a hamburger sound?"

"Fine." It wasn't like she'd taste it anyway.

He collected the hamburger meat and began forming three patties on the counter a few feet from where she sat. He glanced up at her a few times as if about to say something. Finally, he paused, his hands still dug into the meat.

"Jules, if this works...that is, if the senator comes through, it will mean...it will mean that we can be together. In a normal relationship."

She froze, unable to immediately formulate a response. How could she when whatever she said would be a lie? If she told him such a relationship was impossible, he'd demand to know why, and yet she just couldn't commit to the fantasy of them being together when she knew damn well it wasn't going to happen.

"I want that for us, Jules." His eyes burned into her, heating her entire body with their intensity.

She finally looked down, unable to meet his gaze any longer. She'd handled difficult situations before. This shouldn't be any different. But it was. She loved Manny. Had always loved him. And he stood there dangling what she wanted most in the world in front of her.

"What's wrong, Jules?" he asked. "What are you thinking over there?"

"I-I'm just afraid to get my hopes up." It was the first truth she'd uttered in a while. "What if the senator doesn't come through?"

Manny's eyes steeled in determination. "If he doesn't, then we'll find another way. I'm not letting you go."

Her chest tightened at his possessive statement. She shivered lightly. How good it made her feel to know someone loved her so much. How awful she felt to know what she was going to do to that love.

Manny picked up a dish towel and wiped his hands. Then he reached across the bar and cupped her chin. "I need you to trust me, baby. I won't let you go."

She met his gaze. "I do trust you."

His eyes glinted in satisfaction, and he let his hand slide from her face. He returned to making the hamburgers, and she tried to still the flood of panic flowing through her veins.

She'd made her plans while he'd met with the senator. She knew when and how she would leave the townhouse. The rest—proper credentials, the right clothing and other items necessary to complete her mission—Northstar had given her instructions on how to collect. It was all there in the damning e-mail she'd received.

The only thing she didn't know was how she would live with herself when it was all said and done.

"Want to eat at the bar or the table?"

She blinked as Manny's question invaded her thoughts.

"The table is fine."

"Want to set it for me?"

She slid from the barstool and circled around to retrieve plates and silverware from the kitchen.

"You know, I could get used to this," Manny said.

"What's that?"

"You and me in the kitchen. Making meals together. It hints at a rather normal existence."

She heard the hope in his voice. The hope that they would indeed lead a normal life together. She forced a smile to her lips. "Just don't get used to the idea of me cooking."

He laughed. "I'll do the cooking. You can make it up to me in bed." He waggled his eyebrows suggestively.

She turned away before her expression betrayed her. She busied herself setting the round glass table in the small dining area off the kitchen.

A few minutes later, Manny set a platter with the burgers in the middle of the table. "The buns are by the sink. Can you get them?"

She retrieved the buns, then reached for glasses out of the cabinet. "Want ice?" she called.

"Sure."

She set the buns down long enough to open the freezer and fill the glasses with ice. To her surprise, a tear trickled down her cheek. She hurriedly dashed it away, but another slid down to take its place.

She drew in deep steadying breaths in an attempt to compose herself, but they came out in stuttered rasps. God almighty, she was a walking disaster. She was cracking. After three years of being a veritable automaton when it came to her job, she was finally losing it. When it mattered the most.

Her hands shook so hard one of the glasses slipped from her grasp and shattered on the floor.

Manny was beside her in an instant. "Careful. Don't cut yourself." He pulled her away from the shards of glass littering the floor.

She stumbled, her movements stiff and awkward. Tears ran in unending trails down her cheeks.

"Jules, what's wrong?" he demanded.

She stared up at him, knew he was there, but it just didn't register. She was numb from head to toe except for feeling the dampness of the tears slipping over her cheeks. And worse, she was powerless to stop them.

He grasped her by her shoulders and shook her gently. "Jules, snap out of it. What's going on?"

She tried to speak, but her voice caught on a sob, and somewhere deep inside, she splintered. So this was what it felt like when you went crazy. Somehow she expected more violence. Some insane outburst. Not this quiet breakdown.

Manny pulled her into his arms and swayed back and forth as he murmured something unintelligible against her ear. Then he lifted her. Carried her up the stairs. She felt the softness of the bed. God, she was so tired.

He left her for a moment. She heard his voice seemingly miles away. He was on the phone with someone. He sounded concerned.

A moment later, the bed dipped, the covers pulled back. Manny's hard body wrapped protectively around her, his arms sheltering her. She found herself settled against his broad chest.

She lay there for a while, cognizant of the fact that her tears still fell. And yet the most peculiar, wonderful thing had happened. She no longer felt the overwhelming pain she had carried around for so long. She probed inward, trying to rediscover the anguish, the guilt and the fear she lived with. The truth was the only thing she felt was bone-deep fatigue.

She closed her eyes, fully expecting to see the nightmarish visions that had haunted her existence for the last three years. But all she saw was a black void, just what everyone else saw when they closed their eyes.

Relief filtered through her mind. A reprieve from the weight of a million emotions felt to her as if she'd left prison after a long stint in solitary confinement. She liked this weightless floaty feeling.

She snuggled deeper into Manny's arms, arms that tightened protectively around her. Then she simply let go.

Chapter Twenty-Three

She'd been sleeping for eighteen hours, and Manuel was worried. He slouched further into the too-small chair he'd carried up so he could keep watch on Jules. She'd slept all yesterday afternoon, all of last night and through this morning. Without so much as a twitch.

He'd talked to Tony about taking her to a hospital, but their hands were tied until he knew for sure Jules would be safe. He couldn't take her out in public. Too many people were after her. His own agency for one.

So he'd sat and waited. Now they were just a day away, *one* day, from a meeting that could change their lives for the better. Or the worse.

He sighed and scrubbed his face tiredly with one hand. He hadn't slept a damn wink all night. How could he when the woman he loved was falling apart and he was powerless to help her?

More and more he was giving thought to taking Jules out of the country if the senator didn't come through. He couldn't stand by and watch her suffer for crimes she'd been forced to commit, even if it meant turning his back on everything he believed.

Somewhere warm, carefree, and more importantly with no extradition agreement with the U.S.

He hoped like hell it didn't come to that, but he had to face reality. It could. And if it did, he needed to be prepared. He needed to talk to Jules about it, but he wasn't sure how much she could handle right now. She could break at any moment. She *had* broken.

He jerked his head up when he heard her stir. Her eyes fluttered open, and he surged forward out of his chair.

"Jules?" he said softly. He didn't want to alarm her.

She blinked a few times then stared at him with empty eyes. "How long have I slept?" she asked hoarsely.

"It's nearly nine a.m."

"You mean I slept the entire day? Yesterday I mean." Her brow wrinkled in confusion, and her eyes grew cloudier.

He smoothed a hand over her forehead, trying to ease the tension ingrained there. "How do you feel?"

She pursed her lips and appeared to consider his question. "I don't feel much of anything."

Alarm shot through him. She wasn't there. Jules was there on the bed in front of him, but she simply wasn't there. She was someplace else, and damned if he knew where. It scared the hell out of him.

"Want a bath?" he asked softly.

She didn't say anything for a long while, then finally she nodded.

"Wait here. I'll go run the water."

He walked into the bathroom, panic swelling in his chest. How could he reach her? Get past the fog and shadows surrounding her? And what had pushed her over the edge?

When the tub was filled, he went back into the bedroom to find her sitting on the edge of the bed, her legs dangling over the side. She looked lost. And extremely vulnerable. Not even when she was lying in a hospital bed had she looked so defeated.

He knelt in front of her and took her hands in his. "Jules, are you okay?"

Her blue eyes focused on him. She blinked rapidly as if banishing cobwebs. Then she offered him a tremulous smile. "I'm fine."

He put a finger to her forehead and gently rubbed across her head. "What's going on in there, baby?"

Quiet despair was reflected in the soulful pools of her eyes. "I don't know. I feel so...so *disconnected*."

He cupped her shoulders in his hands. "Why don't you go take a long hot bath? I'll make breakfast and bring it up. You can eat in bed. It might be a good idea for you to take it easy today."

She rose unsteadily to her feet. He slipped an arm around her waist to anchor her then walked her into the bathroom.

She managed a half smile. "I'll be fine now."

"You sure?"

She nodded and began to shrug out of her T-shirt. His T-shirt. He leaned forward and kissed her on the top of her head. "I won't be long."

He watched long enough for her to step into the water and settle down, then he headed downstairs.

Jules slid further down into the water and closed her eyes. Whatever had happened yesterday had done a real number on her. She'd never felt so completely empty in her life. Was this what death was like? Complete and utter disembodiment?

Her hand made swirls in the water as she dragged her fingers along the surface. She wasn't complaining. A break from the overwhelming pain and guilt was welcome. She felt about a hundred pounds lighter. And the truth was, she had little to no chance of pulling off her job in the condition she'd been in.

Emotional wrecks didn't make for good assassins.

Her head lolled to the side, the strain of holding it up too much. She studied her toes, the only portion of her lower body above the surface of the water. She wriggled them then continued to stare stoically at them.

Manny's return surprised her. Had she been lying in the tub that long? Concern was engraved on his face as he studied her. Did he expect her to run screaming from the bathroom? Pull her hair out or start frothing at the mouth?

The thought amused her, and she heard herself laugh. Manny only looked more concerned.

Snap out of it, Jules. If you keep this up, he's going to put you on a one-way bus to the funny farm. Then how will you protect him?

"Breakfast ready?" She was proud of the normal tone of her voice. At his nod, she shoved herself up, water running in rivulets down her body.

He took her hand and helped her out, promptly wrapping a towel around her. As if she were a piece of precious porcelain, he dried her and guided her out of the bathroom.

She sat on the bed while he rummaged for her clothing, then she pondered the absurdity of a grown woman having her lover dress her. But doing it herself promised to take more effort than she was willing to expend.

He helped her into a pair of sweats and a T-shirt then set about drying her hair with the towel. When he was finished, he urged her into bed and retrieved the tray he'd set on the dresser.

A plate piled high with biscuits, eggs and bacon wavered in front of her, but the idea of food didn't remotely appeal. Still, she forced a few bites down in an effort to ease the worry she saw on Manny's face.

When she'd had all she could stand, she shoved the plate away and sank back into the pillows behind her. She closed her eyes wearily, wondering how she could possibly be tired when she'd just woken from an eighteen-hour sleep-fest.

Manny tucked the covers around her then lay beside her, pulling her tightly into his arms. She rested her cheek on his chest and closed her eyes. No pain. No horrible oppressive guilt. She'd forgotten what it was like to just sleep.

The beating of Manny's heart and the up-and-down motion of his hand on her back lulled her into a comfortable void. She let it suck her in, gave herself over to the blackness. Damn, it felt good.

She opened her eyes, a peculiar sense of purpose tightening every one of her senses. Manny was gone, and a quick check of the bedside digital clock told her it was time to prepare.

She sat up and swung her legs over the side of the bed. She was alert, her senses heightened. She probed inwardly, wondering what she would find. The assassin. One who had a job to complete in a little over twelve hours.

She strained her ears for any sound of Manny. The vague clinking of dishes told her he was in the kitchen. She stood up and retrieved her bag. Inside the lining of the bag, she withdrew a small vial. A potent drug designed to render the victim senseless for at least eight hours. She'd give it to Manny before bed.

She strode into the bathroom and smoothed her hair behind her ears. Examining herself in the mirror, she was relieved to see a cool, poised woman, not a scared, witless waif.

She bent and splashed cold water on her face then patted her cheeks dry with a hand towel. She tucked the vial in her underwear and smoothed the sweats. A quick look in the mirror reassured her that nothing was visible. Now to go find Manny and put to rest any fears he'd need to commit her.

As she thumped down the stairs, she marveled at how composed she felt. Not being a victim to her raging emotions was exceptionally freeing. She had no idea why she'd snapped, but she was grateful she had. Maybe she was going insane. Maybe she was already there. It didn't matter. As long as she could complete her task.

Manny turned around when he she entered the kitchen. "Jules!" He put down the plate he held and enfolded her in his arms. "How are you feeling?"

"Better," she replied. No lie there. She felt positively wonderful. Who said being a cold, calculating bitch didn't have its plusses? It sure beat the hell out of the alternative.

He pulled away, and relief shone starkly in his eyes. "Glad to hear it. Are you hungry? You didn't eat much this morning."

"Starving," she lied. But how better to convince him she was a-okay than to shovel down a decent meal?

She sat down at the small table and he set something in front of her that resembled spaghetti. She dug into it with false gusto and forced it down her throat. He took the seat across from her and nodded approvingly as she ate.

They ate in silence for several minutes. Finally Manny set his glass of water down after a big gulp and looked over at her.

"What happened, baby?" he asked quietly.

Her cheeks burned under his scrutiny. How was she supposed to explain something she didn't know herself? She didn't try. "I don't know."

He reached across the table and laid his hand over hers. He squeezed lightly. "When this is over, Jules, you and I are going to go somewhere. Somewhere you can rest."

She nodded, mildly surprised his statement didn't send a tsunami of guilt crashing over her. Yep, she'd lost it. Maybe what she had to look forward to *was* a psych ward complete with an I-love-me jacket.

She looked down to see most of her food gone, much to her relief. She put her fork down and leaned back in her chair. "Thank you."

He smiled. "Why don't you go into the living room? I'll clean up and join you. We can watch a movie or something."

Domesticity at its finest. She returned his smile and stood up. "Sure you don't want some help?"

"No, you go ahead."

She shrugged and walked into the living room. She sank down on the couch and curled her feet underneath her. The remote to the television was just a few inches away, but she left it, preferring the silence.

Manny arrived a few minutes later holding two glasses of wine.

"I thought we could both use a relaxing evening," he said as he offered the wine.

She took the glass and sipped obligingly. He sat down beside her and wrapped an arm around her, pulling her against his side.

For a while neither spoke. Manny seemed content to simply hold her and sip the wine. She relaxed against him and let her mind soar above her impending preoccupation. These were the last hours she'd spend in his arms.

"Jules, I wanted to talk to you."

She shifted so she could look up at him.

"This probably isn't the best time, but time isn't something we have a lot of."

She frowned. "What is it?"

He sighed and leaned forward to set his glass on the coffee table. He sank back and stared up at the ceiling.

"I've given this a lot of thought. If for some reason...if for some reason things don't work out with the senator, I want us to go away."

Her brow wrinkled. What he suggested couldn't have surprised her more. "What do you mean by *away*?"

"Out of the country," he said, turning his gaze from the ceiling to her. "Someplace you'd be safe."

She shook her head. Despite the fact she could agree to anything and it wouldn't matter, the mere idea of Manny doing something so contrary to his nature made her ill.

He placed a finger over her lips before she could voice her objections. "It's not up for debate, Jules. There's no way I'm leaving you, and no way I'd keep you somewhere you'd be at risk."

She sighed. She wasn't going to argue with him on their last night, and certainly not over a moot point. She wouldn't be around to leave the country, though that was precisely what she planned to do. Alone.

She glanced at the clock and mentally calculated how much time she needed Manny to be out. If she gave him the drug now, she should have plenty of time to leave the townhouse unnoticed.

"Want some more wine?"

"I'll get it," he said, sitting forward.

She shoved him back then leaned down and kissed him. "I'll get it. You stay here."

She collected his glass from the coffee table and walked into the kitchen. She glanced back to make sure he hadn't followed her then dug out the vial from her underwear.

She dumped the liquid into Manny's wine glass and then poured wine on top of it. A flick of her wrist and the liquid swirled around the glass, effectively mixing the contents. She refilled her own glass then returned to the living room.

He took it from her and took a sip. She sat beside him, and he looked at her with warm eyes.

"I'm glad you're feeling better. You scared the hell out of me."

"I'm sorry," she said softly. "I didn't mean to worry you."

He leaned forward and kissed her before sitting back and sipping his wine again. She relaxed and waited for him to finish. She'd suggest they go to bed soon. After all, they had a big day tomorrow. Their meeting with the senator was to take place in the afternoon. A meeting that would never happen.

Chapter Twenty-Four

Jules woke at four a.m. She immediately turned to see how solidly Manny was sleeping. The drug she had given him shouldn't wear off for a few more hours yet, which gave her plenty of time to make good her escape.

She dressed in silence, donning black jeans and a black T-shirt. She collected the items she needed from her bag—the phone, her Glock and an extra gun clip. Shoving the gun in her waistband, she slipped into the bathroom to check her e-mail once more.

It wasn't like Northstar to be so coy about her target. She waited patiently as she went through the necessary channels to ensure the security of her connection then clicked on the waiting message.

Her mouth rounded into an "O" of shock when she read the name of the man she was supposed to kill. *Senator Adam Denison.* What was Northstar playing at? Did he know of Manny's meeting with the senator? Of course he would. He had been monitoring their movements at all times. Her heart sank. It was further proof of the impossible situation she and Manny were mired in. There was no way out, no matter how hard Manny tried to save her.

She frowned. Manny had said the senator wanted to bust the NFR. Could it be that Northstar feared what the senator would find out if he delved too deep into the organization? It was one possibility. The other was that Northstar was retaliating for Manny seeking the senator's help. A show of power and a sign to Jules that he owned her soul and could get to Manny any time he wished. Maybe it was both. So now, instead of removing a threat to U.S. security as her hits had been in the past, she would be assassinating a man who had the power to expose Northstar and his connection to the U.S. government.

She closed her eyes and replayed the last lines of the e-mail in her head.

Don't think of backing out, Magalie. You wouldn't like the consequences.

She opened her eyes and looked coldly at her reflection in the mirror. "What are you waiting for, assassin? You've got a job to do."

She left the bathroom then went to the window to see if their babysitters still resided in the spot they had been in when she and Manny had gone to bed last night.

The same unmarked car sat across the street. She knew the two agents would alert Tony and Manny the minute they saw her, so first she'd have to make sure they were out of commission.

In this case, there wasn't a whole lot of need for subterfuge. So she'd take the direct route and just approach the agents.

She let herself out the front door and walked across the street to the car. The street was mostly dark. The street lights were spaced far enough not to illuminate the entire area, but she could see clearly. The agents were either sleeping or they didn't think she was a threat. Only when she was staring into the window did they see her.

She drew her gun and pointed it directly at the man in the passenger seat and motioned for him to roll his window down. He looked at her in shock but readily complied.

"Hands where I can see them, gentlemen."

They both raised their hands.

"The radio, cell phones and any wires you have. Out the window."

Reluctantly, they reached down and picked up a collection of cell phones, radios and other devices then pitched them out the window at her feet.

She stepped back then motioned with the gun. "Get out. Both of you."

With exasperated sighs, they stepped out of the car, their hands still in the air.

"We were supposed to be protecting you, not protecting ourselves from you," one of them said acidly.

"Your mistake," she said with a shrug. "Now move. Around back."

She prodded them around to the back of the townhouse. Out of sight of the street, which would be bustling with cars in a few hours. Once they were in the small enclosed backyard, she made them kneel down.

She could see the fear in their faces. Fear that she would kill them. In the past she would have. Would have killed anyone who could compromise her cover. But it didn't matter. After today, there would be no need for anonymity. Manny would know who had assassinated the senator, and she wouldn't be safe anywhere.

"Get it over with," one of the men growled.

She struck him on the back of the head with the butt of her pistol. He slumped forward, unconscious. She registered the surprise on the second agent's face seconds before she rendered him unconscious as well.

She put her gun away and hurried around front. She wasted no time getting into the agents' car and starting the engine. She had two hours to collect her clothing and credentials, reach the target location and get set up for the hit. She wouldn't think beyond that.

Manuel woke with a roaring headache and a swollen tongue. He stumbled from bed into the bathroom and stuck his head under the faucet to wet his mouth. After taking several long swallows, he turned the faucet off and shook his head to clear the cobwebs. What the hell kind of truck ran over him?

A prickle of unease raced up his spine as he processed the fact he had woken alone in the bed. He stuck his head back out of the bathroom to confirm that Jules wasn't there.

He raced down the stairs, looking left and right into the living room and kitchen.

"Jules!" Damn it, she wasn't anywhere to be found, and his head felt like someone had taken a sledgehammer to it.

He went to the back door and flung it open to see if she was out on the small patio. What he saw made his blood turn to ice.

He ran over to the two men lying on the ground. He placed his fingers to the first man's neck and breathed a sigh of relief when he felt a strong pulse. After doing the same to the second man, Manuel determined he was alive as well.

After a moment's hesitation, he ran back inside and up the stairs to retrieve his cell phone. He punched in Tony's number as he ran back down to the unconscious men.

"It's early," Tony complained in a bleary voice.

"I need an ambulance," Manuel bit out.

"What?" Tony's voice lost any semblance of fogginess.

"The two agents. They're out cold in my backyard. And Jules is gone."

"Oh shit."

"I've got to find her. I've got to find out what the hell happened here."

"I'll get the ambulance rolling. Sit tight, I'll be right over."

Manuel flipped the phone closed and knelt by the agents. He lightly tapped one on the cheek. "Come on, man, wake up. I need you here."

After a few minutes, the agent stirred and uttered a low groan.

"That's it," Manuel encouraged. "Wake up."

The agent's eyes fluttered open, closed, then opened again. "Damn, my head hurts."

"Yours and mine both," Manuel said with a grunt. "What's your name?"

"Agent Matthews." He struggled up and then bent to check on his partner. "Come on, Eddie, wake the hell up." He shook his partner until he uttered a sound of protest.

"Damn bitch clobbered us both," Matthews said.

Manuel froze. "What did you say?"

Eddie sat up, rubbing the back of his neck. Matthews helped him to his feet.

"The woman you've been shacked up with here," Matthews said darkly. "She pulled a gun on us, led us back here then cold-cocked us."

Manuel's hands began to tremble. A multitude of sensations, all of which were unpleasant, coursed through his body with the speed of a locomotive.

"You both should come in and sit down. I've called for an ambulance."

"We'll sit, but no ambulance," Eddie muttered. "Embarrassing enough to be taken by a slip of a girl. Guys at headquarters would never let us live down a trip to the hospital."

Manuel picked up his phone to call Tony. "Cancel the ambulance."

"I'm almost there," Tony said. "The agents are all right, I take it?"

"Yeah, they're fine. I'll talk to you when you get here."

He closed the phone. Then he rammed his fist into the wall. He ignored the explosion of pain and hit it again. Plaster rained down on the floor.

"Hey man, cool it. You're going to break your hand," Matthews cautioned.

Manuel turned to glare at the two agents sitting on the couch. "Why the hell didn't you stop her?"

Eddie glared back at him. "She had a gun pointed at us. What the hell were we supposed to do? I thought she was going to kill us."

"What did she say? I need to know every detail, no matter how small."

Eddie gave him a disgruntled look. "We were two hours from the next shift taking over. We were tired. Nothing was going on. Then all of a sudden your girl shows up pointing a gun at the car window. She made us throw out the radios and phones then had us get out of the car. She took us around back, forced us to kneel down, then she knocked us out. End of story."

"She said nothing else?"

Eddie shook his head.

They all jerked around when they heard the door open. Tony walked into the living room holding an array of electronic devices.

"These belong to you guys?" he drawled as he looked over at Matthews and Eddie.

"Yeah, they're ours," Eddie muttered.

"Well, except that one." Matthews pointed at one of the phones.

"Which one?" Tony asked.

Matthews walked over to where Tony was standing and took one of the phones. "This one."

Tony turned it over in his hand, examining it. He looked up at Manuel. "So what's going on?"

"She drugged me," Manuel said bleakly. "She fucking drugged me, knocked out the agents and took off."

He felt an overwhelming urge to put his fist through the wall again.

Tony had opened the phone and began punching a series of buttons. "Quite a piece of technology. You sure this doesn't belong to one of you?" he asked the agents.

"No, she must have dropped it when we got out of the car," Eddie replied.

After several minutes, Tony's brow furrowed, then he held out the phone to Manuel. "You better read this, man. It'll explain where your girl was going in such a hurry."

Manuel took the phone and held it up. He scrolled through the message, rage flowing like a wild current through his body.

"When you're done with that one, hit the next button," Tony said. "It gets better."

When Manuel read the next message and saw the name of the intended target, he nearly exploded. The man who had promised to help, the man who could very well have arranged a normal life for him and Jules, was the man she was going to kill.

He started to throw the phone across the room, but Tony grabbed his arm and retrieved the phone. "I'm not finished with that."

"I've got to stop her," Manuel said. "Before it's too late. Call out whoever you need, but get everyone you can to the Ronald Reagan Center pronto. I can't let her do it. I'm going to have to take her down."

"I know, man," Tony said quietly. "And I'm sorry."

"We'll go with you," Matthews said.

"No."

Tony threw Manuel the keys. "Use my car. I'll get someone over here to pick me and the boys up."

Manuel yanked on his shoulder holster then shoved his gun into place. He ran out to Tony's car and climbed in. Seconds later, he careened down the street, driving as fast as he could.

"Damn it, Jules!"

He pounded the steering wheel. How could she turn her back on everything he was offering her? How could she betray him, take everything they'd shared, their past, their future and gut him with it?

She had played him from day one. Used him to get to D.C. so she could carry out her damn assignment. Everything she'd done, everything she'd said, had been a complete *lie*. He'd never been so goddamn angry in his entire life.

He arrived at the Ronald Reagan International Trade Center in record time. He roared up to the front and leaped out of the car. A dozen agents met him, guns drawn. He yanked out his ID and bolted for the entrance.

An FBI agent stopped him as he hit the door.

"What the hell is going on here?" the agent demanded.

"There's going to be an attempt on Senator Denison's life. I need to know if anyone new showed up for duty this morning. A woman."

The agent frowned then snapped his fingers. "Yes, Kerry McDonald. Impeccable record. I called in about her myself. She was brought in for this assignment especially. A top-notch sniper. She's on the upper level pulling guard duty."

Manuel didn't wait to hear more. He ran for the stairs leading to the balcony. There in the atrium, Senator Denison's name was being announced as the next speaker. Manuel prayed he would make it in time.

Chapter Twenty-Five

Jules relaxed her tightly wound body and shouldered her rifle. The speaker had droned on for several minutes. The senator should be coming to the podium shortly.

This was by far the easiest assignment she'd ever been handed. So easy that she felt a sense of foreboding. With the FBI badge and the fabricated background Northstar had arranged, walking into the building and getting past the Secret Service detail had been simple.

Here she was on sniper watch. Her job? To take out any threat to the senator. She nearly laughed. She *was* the threat to the senator, and all she had to do was wait for him to take the stage and pick him off.

Northstar had made it so easy, anyone could have done the job. So why was he so adamant that she do it? It didn't make sense. But then nothing that twisted bastard did made sense.

The seconds ticked by, and her cool exterior began to falter. The numbness she'd embraced began to wear off as she imagined the consequences of what she was about to do.

She closed her eyes and thought of Manny, who by now must know of her betrayal. He would be furious. And hurt. But at least he didn't know what she was about to do. He wouldn't know until she was well away and out of his life. Maybe he'd never know. She'd disappear just as she had three years ago, only this time it would be of her own volition.

Was she doing the right thing? She shook her head. No, but then the right thing wouldn't save Manny. Manny the protector, the enforcer. Would he want to live knowing she'd paid for his life in blood?

She heard the speaker's voice through the small microphone she wore in her ear. He was announcing the senator's name. She adjusted the rifle on her shoulder and leaned forward to look through the scope at the man she was supposed to kill.

When she finally put the cross hairs on him, she nearly dropped the rifle in her shock. Bile rose in her throat. Her stomach rolled violently. Sweat broke out on her forehead, and she swallowed convulsively.

Her hands shook until she had to veer her head away from the scope. The *bastard.* The bastard who had raped her, who had forced her to join the CIA's shadow group called the NFR, who had been the man behind Northstar three years ago. He stood before her, smiling at the assembled crowd. Senator Adam Denison, the man in line for the post of Director of Homeland Security, was the worst sort of criminal.

She settled the cross hairs back on him, her pulse pounding loudly in her head. She drew in a deep breath then let it out slowly. Her hands steadied themselves, and her finger curled around the trigger. He deserved to die. She wanted to be the one to send him to hell.

"Drop the rifle, Jules."

She froze in horror as Manny's cold voice rushed over her.

"Do it now. Don't make me shoot you."

She raised her head from the scope then slowly turned to look over her shoulder. Manny stood pointing his gun at her, anger etched on every surface of his face.

She let her hand fall from the trigger then rolled over on her back, putting her hands up where he could see them.

His eyes glittered dangerously as he advanced on her. He reached down for the rifle then backed away.

"Why, Jules? Why would you do it?"

She swallowed.

"No, don't answer," he cut in before she could speak. "I don't care. Get up."

She scrambled up, watching him warily. Her heart ached at the hatred she saw in his eyes. She didn't know how he'd found her, found out what she was doing, but she knew he'd never forgive her.

"I thought I could take you down. I came here to arrest you for the terrorist you are, but when it comes down to it, I just can't."

She opened her mouth to speak, but he shook his head angrily.

"Not a word. Not a damn word. I'm not interested in anything you have to say. You've told enough lies to last a lifetime."

He looked at her with disgust that turned to sorrow, deep sadness swimming in his eyes.

"Walk away, Jules. God knows I should take you in so they can throw the book at you, but I can't do it. But know this. If I ever see you, if I ever so much as think you're in the vicinity, I'll take you in so fast your head will spin. You run and you keep running."

She stared at him, stunned by his words.

"What are you waiting for? Get the hell out of here. I'd do it before Tony shows up and explains the situation to the feds."

She turned and ran, her heart breaking the entire way. When she descended the stairs, she slowed, donning a cool expression. She strode out the front as if she owned the place, but inside she was a mess.

Manny had managed to break through the numbness. She felt, oh how she felt. She felt every single word he'd thrown at her. To the very depths of her soul.

She walked past countless agents, through the cars in the parking lot and down the street that had since been cordoned off. She flashed her badge at the cops who started to stop her at the barricade and they stepped aside to let her pass.

She walked until the building was no longer in sight, and she never looked back. There was nothing there for her. She kept walking until the wind blew cold on her wet cheeks.

And then a stronger sense of grief struck her. She hadn't killed the senator. Northstar, whatever his purposes, wouldn't care why. He would strike back at her, ruthlessly, without mercy. Manny would die, and all because she had hesitated. She had let her emotions take over in that single minute, and Manny would pay for it with his life.

She curled her fingers into tight fists. Whatever power struggle had erupted between Northstar and the senator, the only clear solution to the problem was to take Northstar out.

She needed to lure him into the open. What happened to her as a result, she didn't care. This one last thing she would do for Manny, for her parents and for the girl she had once been.

Chapter Twenty-Six

Manuel swigged down another beer and tossed the bottle into the growing collection on the floor in front of him. He eyed the empty carton in disgust then reached past it for the unopened bottle of whiskey.

After fumbling with the lid, he tilted it back and let the fire pour down his throat. He coughed and wiped at his mouth with the back of his hand.

Beer before liquor, never sicker.

The old adage swam around in his brain, and he emitted a harsh laugh. It wasn't possible for him to be any sicker than he already was.

His chest hurt, his head hurt, his *heart* hurt. And he'd never been so goddamn mad in his life.

For two days, he'd sat in this chair, drinking, trying to drink himself into a coma. He'd barely slept, and when he had, his dreams had been little more than a reenactment of his last scene with Jules.

Damn her. Damn her to hell and the bloody NFR along with her. What had they done to her to instill such loyalty that she would turn her back on someone she purported to love? Had she ever loved him? He hadn't thought anyone could be that good an actress, but now he wondered. She'd certainly played him like a fiddle.

He swallowed back more whiskey and prayed for oblivion to claim him. Maybe then he wouldn't hurt so damn much.

A rapid staccato sounded at the door to his apartment.

"Fuck off," Manuel muttered.

The knocking grew louder, and Manuel tilted the bottle back some more.

Finally it stopped, and he slammed the bottle back down again.

"What the hell are you doing to yourself?" Tony asked in disgust. At least he thought it was Tony. To be honest, it sounded as though he were underwater.

He opened one eye and peered across the room in the direction of the voice. Tony stood in the doorway of the living room, glaring—what the hell did he have to be pissed at, anyway?

"Get the fuck out of here," Manuel demanded.

Tony crossed the room and came to stand a few feet from where Manuel sat slouched in his armchair.

"Look, dude. I don't have a lot of time, and I need your full attention. Haul your ass upstairs, take a shower and sober up. Then get back down here because there are some things you need to hear."

Manuel studied him with half-closed eyes. "Tony, I don't really give a rat's ass. Get the hell out of my house. I quit."

"No, you aren't quitting yet." Tony jerked a thumb toward the stairs. "Get going or so help me, I'll throw you in the shower myself."

"You and what army?" Manuel grumbled. But he shoved himself up and made his way unsteadily toward the stairs.

"I'll make you some coffee," Tony offered. "Looks like you could use a pot. Or two."

Manuel waved in irritation. Whatever it took to make him go away.

He slugged his way up the stairs, walked into the bathroom, shed his clothing and stepped directly into the cold spray. He sucked in his breath in shock as it hit him full-on. He stuck his head under the water and let it slosh down his back.

For five minutes, he stood there, his hands braced on the shower wall, head bent, eyes closed. When his head began to clear, he fumbled for the knobs and turned the water off.

Whatever it was Tony had to tell him, it couldn't be any worse than what had already happened. His estimation of Jules certainly couldn't be any lower, so he had nothing to lose by listening to the all-important information.

He yanked on a T-shirt, collected a pair of jeans and hopped out of the room on one leg as he thrust the other one into the pants.

When he arrived downstairs, Tony shoved a steaming mug of coffee into his hands. "Drink it," his partner ordered.

Manuel sat on the couch and plunked the cup down in front of him on the coffee table. "Okay, what's so important that you'd come all the way over here to tell me? Thought that was what the phone was for."

"You needed to hear this in person," Tony said.

Manuel leaned back and sighed. "All right, out with it then."

Tony reached into his coat pocket and pulled out Jules's phone. Manuel's gut tightened.

"I played around with this quite a bit," Tony began. "The only messages I found stored were the ones you already saw. And there were no records of phone numbers from incoming or outgoing calls. But what I did find were dates and times she received calls."

Manuel continued to stare at him. "And this is important why?"

"I'm getting to that," Tony said impatiently. "I fed the information into our database of phone conversations, but there are millions upon millions of conversations to sort through, and with only a date and a time, the likelihood of getting a hit is slim to none. So I had to narrow the search parameters. Think of words that might have been used, not very common words if we were going to come up with a short list."

Manuel drummed his fingers, waiting for his partner to get to the point. Assuming he had one.

"I tried all sorts of words a man might use when ordering an assassination, but everything I tried came up with no less than a hundred thousand possibilities. Again, not good when time is a factor."

Tony's voice went up in excitement. Despite his attempt at disinterest, Manuel leaned forward.

"I noticed in both of the e-mails on Jules's phone, the man she calls Northstar has a habit of calling her Magalie. So I tried Magalie, used the dates and times of the phone calls Jules received, then weeded through a few thousand French conversations and came across this."

He reached forward and placed a digital recorder on the coffee table. He pressed the play button with his thumb and stood back.

Manuel flinched when Jules's wavery voice filtered out of the recorder.

"You don't need me anymore. Why won't you just let me go?"

"Oh, but I do need you, Magalie. One last time."

Manuel's stomach rolled as he listened to the exchange. Jules sounded so small. Defeated. Then fury washed over him with the next words.

"If you refuse, you can kiss your little boyfriend goodbye. Don't fuck with me. You know what I'm capable of. Removing lover boy from the picture would be nothing more than swatting an insect with a flyswatter..."

"Do this assignment, and you'll have what you most want. Your freedom. Refuse and I'll make your life a living hell. Maybe you remember what happened the first time you hesitated."

Manuel lost Jules's responses. He focused solely on the bastard taunting her. He knew that voice. But it couldn't be. It simply could not *be*.

"Or maybe you liked it? Did you enjoy it, Magalie?"

Then Jules's tired, defeated voice. Full of resignation.

"I'll do it."

Tony reached down and shut off the recorder. Then he stared hard at Manuel. "This is only the beginning, Manuel. Are you prepared to hear the rest?"

"Jesus Christ, Tony! That sounded like Sanderson."

"It was. It is."

Manuel's mouth dropped open. It was incomprehensible. What the hell was the director of Manuel and Tony's counter-terrorism unit, a man Manuel had trusted, called a *friend*, doing threatening Jules into assassinating a United States senator?

Chapter Twenty-Seven

Patience was rewarded. Jules knew this. And on the second day of her vigil, she knew her time had come.

She'd come to this secluded garden adjoining the National Cathedral, numb with the depth of her despair. Fueled by the need for revenge, driven to protect Manny with her last breath. And it could well mean the end of her.

She curled her fingers around the cold stock of her gun and waited. Waited for the senator to make his appearance.

The sun was sinking lower in the sky. Only a few hours of daylight remained, yet she knew he would come. Her phone call to the senator's office would not go ignored. Whether Northstar would accompany him was anyone's guess, but the senator was a good place to start in her quest for vengeance.

She sucked in the cold air, let it wash over her, then breathed it out again in a visible puff. She knew it was near freezing, and yet she didn't feel any discomfort. The light jacket she wore was not for warmth, it was to disguise her weapon.

She stared rigidly over the spiraling pathways, waiting for the senator to appear. She'd shoot the bastard, but first she'd make him tell her where she could find Northstar.

Over the last three years, she'd wondered what it would take to completely turn her into the cold-blooded monster she feared. Now she knew. Her transformation was complete. Gone was the girl who felt each kill to her depths, each one chipping away at her soul. She embraced this kill. This one would set her free.

She rocked slightly, the movement soothing, helping her focus on the task at hand. Unbidden images of Manny streaked through her mind. Instantly she was bombarded with pictures of what her life might have been like had Northstar and the senator never crossed her path.

She rocked faster.

More time passed and still no sign of the senator. As the sun dipped lower into the horizon, she continued her vigil. Then, as the shadows crept across the bench where she sat, she saw him.

"Yeah, that was my reaction, too," Tony said grimly. "But it's him. After I heard this conversation, I did some digging. I haven't slept since I don't know when."

"Join the club," Manuel muttered. He ran a hand through his hair. "I don't understand any of it."

"I don't think it's possible to understand the extent your lives were manipulated," Tony said, a whisper of amazement in his voice.

Manuel stared hard at him. Manipulated? Somehow he knew he was about to embark on a twisted journey, one that was going to shake the foundations of everything he thought was true. And that scared the hell out of him.

"Spill it," he demanded.

Tony paced back and forth in front of the couch. "First of all, Jules's name really is Magalie. Magalie Pinson. Her parents were indeed Frederic and Carine Pinson. They were French immigrants who settled in the U.S. right out of college. The CIA recruited them for a top-secret shadow group they labeled the NFR."

"*What?*" Manuel demanded. "The NFR is a CIA brainchild? But it's a terrorist group!"

Tony shook his head. "Think about it, Manuel. A group assembled by the CIA under the guise of a terrorist cell. They do the dirty work for the CIA and the CIA takes none of the blame. Think state-sponsored assassination, only on a larger scale. The NFR could take out targets that would be a political nightmare for the U.S. to get involved with."

Manuel shook his head in denial. God, it couldn't be true.

"I hacked into Sanderson's computer. Took me all damn night, but I was successful. Bastard had extensive logs dating back from the NFR's inception. Dates, names, targets—you name it, he had them listed. Apparently the NFR was formed in the late sixties, but they didn't become very active until the early eighties when someone he referred to as FAAID, and later as SAID, took over."

"But why Jules?" Manuel asked, his head spinning. "If she was the Pinsons' daughter, how did I find her all those years ago? And my recruitment—I refuse to believe that's coincidental."

Tony shook his head in regret. "No, it wasn't, Manny. You and Jules have been manipulated for years. For whatever reason, the Pinsons wanted out, only FAAID wasn't having it. The Pinsons disappeared, taking their daughter with them. I'm assuming they must have abandoned Jules or maybe they were killed. I wasn't able to find any information as to how Jules ended up on your street twenty-three years ago. But Sanderson discovered Jules was the Pinsons' daughter when she was ten.

The Trehans had her fingerprinted as part of an abduction awareness campaign."

Tony paused and turned to look at Manuel. "Whoever FAAID is, apparently he was livid over the Pinsons' defection. He directed Sanderson to set into motion the events that later transpired in France when Jules visited after graduating college."

"And my recruitment? Sanderson recruited me personally."

Tony nodded, his expression grim. "He recruited you so he would have something to control Jules with."

"Son of a bitch!"

Manuel stood, clenching his fist. God, he wanted to kill someone. They'd been puppets. For the last fifteen years, they'd been nothing but laboratory mice under a microscope. Jules had never had a chance.

"And Manuel, her recruitment story. It was true. Every bit of it. Sanderson has a rather detailed account of just what they did to make sure she complied with their wishes."

Disgust dripped from Tony's voice. Manuel knew well what he must have found. He wanted to puke.

He closed his eyes, seized with the enormity of his error. A mistake had never felt bigger than this one.

"Oh my God, Tony," he choked out. "I sent her away."

"At least you didn't feed her to the sharks," Tony said. "Your instincts were good. You let her go."

"I let her go because I love her, and I didn't have the balls to cuff her and turn her over to the feds. Not because I *believed* in her."

He closed his eyes. He *hadn't* believed in her. He forced his mind back to the details at hand. "Why does Sanderson want the senator dead? Because he was going to help Jules?"

Tony frowned. "I don't really know. There are several mentions that SAID wanted to shut down the NFR and cease operations. Maybe the senator scared them. His stance on terrorism has always been tight, and with his appointment to Homeland Security, he could have exposed the NFR's ties to the CIA, especially if Jules talked."

Manuel's mind raced in a sick pattern. He took in all that Tony had said and tried to put all the pieces together. Who was SAID/FAAID? Whoever he was, he'd been in France three years ago when Jules had taken her trip. He'd lain in wait for her along with Sanderson.

France. SAID. Senator Adam Denison. The name floated in front of him like a beacon. Jesus.

He turned to Tony, his face drawn in horror. "Tony, wasn't the senator once the French ambassador?"

Tony's brow wrinkled in confusion. "Yeah, until two years ago when he won the Senate election."

"French Ambassador Adam Isaac Denison. Senator Adam Isaac Denison."

Tony's eyes registered his understanding. "Holy shit."

"It all makes perfect sense," Manuel said. "The senator, who was then the French ambassador, headed the NFR, a shadow group within the CIA. Imagine how good it would make the senator look to bust the NFR wide open in the early days of his Homeland Security appointment. Sanderson must have resisted the idea of disbanding the group. Which would explain why he wanted Jules to assassinate the senator."

Bile rose in Manuel's throat. Everything she'd done had been to keep him safe. Just like she'd said. And he'd judged her and dismissed her. Guilty. He'd been judge and jury, and he'd convicted her without a second thought.

Panic tightened every nerve ending in his body. Jules wasn't safe. Not from the senator and not from Sanderson.

"I've got to find her."

Tony glanced uneasily at him. "I know where she is."

Manuel's head shot up. "What do you mean you know where she is?"

Tony shifted from one foot to the other and shoved his hands into his pockets. "I kept tabs on her after she left the Ronald Reagan building. I knew you'd let her go, but I thought it in our best interest to monitor her movements."

"So where is she?"

Manuel started for the door, his need to find her overwhelming. He couldn't lose her. Not after all they'd been through. Not after he'd turned his back on her.

"I think she's planning some kind of damn suicide mission."

Manuel spun back around. "What the *fuck* are you talking about?

"For the past two days, she's sat in the same place. All day long. She sits, doesn't move. Just waits for something. Or someone. I think she's waiting for either the senator or Sanderson. Maybe both. I think this is her last stand, so to speak."

Manuel's blood ran cold. "Where, Tony? Tell me where, damn it. I have to get to her before they do."

"The Bishop's Garden. And I'm going with you."

Manuel didn't wait to hear more. He ran from the apartment as fast as he could go. He threw himself into Tony's SUV seconds before Tony barreled into the passenger seat.

He tore down the street, honking at slow traffic, swerving around stopped vehicles. He cursed, he yelled, he was scared to death.

"How far up does this go, Tony? Who can we trust?" Manuel demanded as he maneuvered through the busy streets.

"I'm calling the FBI," Tony muttered. "Screw the CIA."

Several minutes later, the longest of his entire life, Manuel turned into lane leading to the cathedral then slammed on the brakes. "Isn't that Sanderson's car?" He pointed to a gray sedan parked several spaces down from the small entrance to the garden.

Tony jumped out, gun drawn. Manuel slammed the SUV into park and charged out after Tony. Manuel could see someone in the driver's seat, and he motioned Tony to the other side.

Guns raised, they circled around until Manuel had a direct bead on the driver.

He was dead.

Chapter Twenty-Eight

Jules's hand curled tightly around the gun as the senator strode toward her. When he was a few feet away, she stood up, drew the pistol and leveled it at him.

"That's far enough."

Scorn rippled across the senator's face. "Going to kill me, Magalie? I think not. You'd never get away with it."

She shivered as her gaze swept over his sneering visage. She remembered his face well. It was burned into her memory.

"I don't care whether I get away with it or not. Where is Northstar?"

"Dead. Just like you're going to be," the senator said in a cold voice.

Could he be lying? Or had he already gotten to Northstar? It mattered little to her. As long as the bastard was dead.

She stared intently at him. "Why did you do it?"

"Why what? Why recruit you? Why kill Northstar? Blame your parents, Magalie. It was for them that I enjoyed destroying you. I imagined the look on your father's face as I raped you."

Rage swept over Jules. Her finger tightened on the trigger, and she knew in that moment, she could kill him in cold blood. And damn the consequences.

A quiet popping erupted, and for a moment, she thought she'd done it. But no, it wasn't loud enough, and she didn't recall pulling the trigger. Her entire body jerked, and she fell to the ground. Pain arced through her body, ricocheting from her chest, radiating outward with amazing speed.

She blinked in confusion as her gun dropped from numb fingers. Her fingers. She looked up to see the senator holding a gun with a silencer. His image swam, and she blinked again to try and clear the cobwebs.

Her free hand traveled to her chest. She felt wetness, and when she pulled it away, she looked down to see it bright red with her blood.

"Once again you underestimated me. Rest in peace, Magalie. Say hello to your parents for me."

She watched him walk away. In the distance she heard shouting. Her muddled brain tried to make sense of the noise. Manny. He was here.

Oh God, the senator would kill Manny. She couldn't allow it. No. No. No!

Tears leaked down her cheeks. The pain was more than she'd ever endured in her life. She could *feel* her pulse growing weaker. She could feel herself slipping away. She had to get to Manny. Had to save him.

She pulled herself along the ground with her arm, nearly passing out from the agony. Awake. She had to stay awake. She felt the smooth metal of her gun, ran her hand down until she gripped the stock.

Mustering every bit of her strength, she curled her legs underneath her in an attempt to propel herself up. She made it up to her elbow before nearly collapsing. Black dots swirled in her vision, and she blinked furiously to dispel them. She gritted her teeth and forced herself to her knees.

The metallic bite of blood filled her mouth. She forced the panic away. She wouldn't die yet.

With every ounce of her will, all her love for Manny, all the hatred she felt for the senator, she pushed herself upward, nearly exploding from the effort. In the distance she could see the senator. And beyond, she saw Manny racing toward her.

She raised her gun and pointed it at the senator.

Manuel had pulled open the door and touched his fingers to Sanderson's still-warm neck. He was dead, and Manuel didn't have time to waste on the bastard anyway. He'd run for the gardens adjacent to the cathedral.

He'd charged down one of the paths, pausing at the top of the incline to look down over the gardens. His heart had nearly stopped when he saw the senator and Jules. She had a gun pointed at Denison, but suddenly she'd crumpled to the ground.

He shouted her name and started forward. The senator turned around and walked rapidly toward them. Manuel charged forward, his gun raised.

The senator raised his own arm and pointed a silencer at Manuel. A loud shot rang through the air. A look of surprise funneled across Denison's face just as a thin stream of blood trickled out of his mouth. Then he sank to the ground, the gun falling from his hand.

Jules stood in the distance, holding the gun that had just felled the senator. But all Manuel could focus on was the blood. God, there was so much blood on her.

He ran for her as she sank to the ground. His heart pounded furiously. Time slowed. He couldn't get to her fast enough. His damn feet felt like they were encased in cement.

Finally he flung himself to the ground beside her and gathered her in his arms. Blood. There was blood everywhere. Oh God. His throat swelled. Pain lanced through his chest. Despair pounded him relentlessly

"Jules! Jules, wake up, baby. You have to wake up!"

He buried his face in her hair and rocked her back and forth in his arms.

"Goddamn you, Jules. Don't die on me. Don't you dare die."

Sobs welled and tore from his throat. He couldn't breathe. He couldn't think. He couldn't live without her.

He touched her cheek, shook her gently, covered her chest wound with his hands, anything to try and save her. He felt for a pulse and found only the slightest whisper of one in her neck.

"That's it, baby. You hang on," he said fiercely. "I'm not giving you up again."

He gathered her closer in his arms. "Someone get a goddamn ambulance!" he yelled. He'd never felt so damn helpless in his life.

"Manny."

The barest whisper filtered to his ears.

He drew away and saw her eyelids flicker weakly. She'd said his name.

"Jules, sweetheart, I'm here."

She licked her lips, the action seeming to take every ounce of her strength.

"Let me go, Manny," she whispered. "The things…the things I've done. I'm beyond redemption. Just let me go." Her voice cracked and blood bubbled from her mouth.

"Never," he said fiercely. "You're so all-fired determined to protect me. Well, you can't protect me unless you live. Now *fight*, damn it."

An eerie smile curved her lips, completely incongruous with all the blood and the mask of pain she'd worn just seconds ago.

"I smell...vanilla." Her eyelids fluttered weakly, and she stared seemingly beyond him, through him. "Mom? Pop?"

Panic flooded him. "Shhh. Don't talk. Save your strength." He turned and looked back to where Tony stood a few feet away. "Where's the damn ambulance!" Desperation raced up his spine.

She arched her back, her lips working up and down. "I love you." It slipped from her lips in the frailest of whispers. Then she closed her eyes, and her head lolled to the side.

No! No! No! No!

He gripped her tightly to him uncaring of all the blood. "Live, damn it! Don't you give up, Jules. I love you too much to let you go."

Tears streaked down his cheeks.

"Don't leave me," he croaked out.

He was pushed aside as two paramedics bent over her. In quick succession, one of them intubated her while the other started an IV. Within seconds, she was hoisted on a stretcher and hustled into a waiting ambulance.

Manuel stumbled after them, watching as they squeezed oxygen into her lungs with an Ambu bag.

Tony shoved him toward the SUV. "I'll drive you."

"The senator?

"He's being taken to the hospital. He's alive."

"He deserves to die." Manuel only wished he'd done it.

He climbed numbly into the SUV and stared blindly out the window as Tony raced after the ambulance. He'd failed Jules. Not once but twice. Twice he'd not been there when she needed him most. And now she might die because of it.

Chapter Twenty-Nine

Manuel paced the surgery waiting room, about to go insane. She'd been in surgery eight hours. The longest eight hours of his life.

He knew it wasn't good. A bullet to the chest, all the blood she'd lost. But still, he wouldn't allow himself to lose hope, to admit that he might lose her.

Tony had been on the phone nearly the entire time. They hadn't trusted anyone at the CIA. Not over something this big. Hell, they'd had a hard enough time spilling the story to the feds, but they had to trust someone.

He glanced over as Tony got up from his seat, shut his phone and walked over to where Manuel stood.

"They've got warrants for the senator's office and home. I'm going over. I don't want anyone touching his computers but me. I'll let you know what I find out."

Manuel nodded, red fury washing over him all over again. While Jules fought for her life on an operating table, the senator was undergoing surgery to remove a bullet from his shoulder. The bastard was expected to make a full recovery.

He finally sat down, fatigue taking over. He leaned forward and buried his face in his hands, and for the first time in longer than he remembered, he prayed.

He'd lost the Trehans to the senator's machinations. He couldn't lose Jules too. He prayed she wouldn't give up.

Hours came and went and still he sat, refusing to budge. Finally, fifteen hours after Jules had been rushed into surgery, the doctor appeared at the door.

He looked tired, haggard, and worst of all, there was no spark of hope in his eyes.

Tears stung Manuel's eyelids, and he swallowed back a moan of despair as he rose to hear what the doctor would say.

"I'll be honest with you, Mr. Ramirez. I expected her to die in surgery. But she hung on. I have no explanation."

"Will she...will she make it?" Manuel asked, his voice cracking.

"She made it through surgery, so I'd say she has a better than average chance of recovering. She's in ICU, where she'll remain until she's stable. The bullet missed her heart, but she lost an enormous amount of blood. She's got a long recovery ahead of her, but she's made it through the toughest part."

Manuel's heart began to pound. His knees shook and threatened to buckle underneath him.

"Maybe you should sit down." The doctor said gestured toward the chair closest to him.

Manuel sank into the chair and stared at the doctor in disbelief. "She's alive?" He needed to hear it one more time.

The doctor nodded. "She's very fortunate. When she came in, I gave her less than a five percent chance of pulling through. With the amount of blood loss, it didn't seem likely she'd survive the first hour of surgery." He shrugged. "But then in this profession, I've witnessed some pretty amazing things. I'd say Miss Trehan has friends in high places."

"Thank you." Manuel reached out to shake the doctor's hand. "I appreciate all you did for her."

The doctor smiled. "You should get some rest now."

"When can I see her?" Manuel asked, ignoring the doctor's suggestion.

The doctor's face softened. "You can go up to ICU and see her for a few minutes. But I warn you, it will be a shock. We'll have her hooked to a respirator until I'm comfortable she can breathe on her own."

Manuel nodded then got up and walked past the doctor. He followed the signs to the intensive care unit and checked in with the nurse at the desk.

She escorted him back to the corner cubicle. He sucked in his breath when he saw Jules lying there, so still, so pale.

"I'll give you a few minutes," the nurse said. "Then you'll have to come back tomorrow."

Manuel nodded and moved closer to the bed. The respirator echoed eerily in the otherwise quiet space. Jules's chest, heavily bandaged, rose up and down with the sound of the machine.

A series of tubes and wires extended from her to a heart monitor and an IV pump. He could see the steady rhythm of her heart displayed on the small screen. She was alive.

He stood at her bedside and reached down, curling his hand carefully around her fingers. They felt cold. He rubbed her hand soothingly, wanting her to somehow know he was there beside her.

"Jules? Baby, I'm here."

Silence greeted him in response. Only the steady whooshing of the respirator could be heard.

He leaned closer in, afraid to touch her. He brushed his lips lightly across her forehead. "I love you. Come back to me. You're safe now."

A single tear rolled down his cheek, and he sucked in his breath to control the grief that threatened to explode from him.

"Mr. Ramirez," the nurse said softly from the end of the bed. "It's time for you to go now. You can come back tomorrow."

Reluctantly, he removed his hand from Jules's and backed away from the bed. He didn't want to leave her. Not even for a minute.

As he walked with the nurse out of the enclosure, he saw two men standing nearby. His hackles rose, and he stopped in front of them.

"Who are you and why the hell are you here?" he demanded.

"I'm Special Agent Farrow," the first man said. He turned and gestured to the other man. "This is Special Agent Redding. We've been assigned to Ms. Trehan."

Fear churned in Manuel's gut.

"I assume you're Manuel Ramirez?" Agent Redding asked.

Manuel nodded.

Agent Redding stuck out a hand to shake Manuel's. "We've been talking to Tony. He's cooperating with the investigation into the senator's participation in the NFR."

Manuel relaxed.

"We're here to ensure Ms. Trehan's safety," Agent Farrow said.

Manuel studied them for several long seconds. Then he reached for his phone. He wasn't leaving Jules, not until he talked to Tony.

Tony answered on the second ring.

"Tony, there are two guys here. Said you spoke to them. They're assigned to protect Jules?"

"Yeah, sorry, I was going to call you. How is she?"

"She's...she's alive." It was all he could say. "What are the agents' names, and what do they look like?" Manuel asked, staring at the two men standing there.

"Agent Redding and Agent Farrow. Agent Redding is tall, blond hair, medium build. Agent Farrow is shorter, dark hair, mustache, stocky build. You can trust them, Manuel." Tony paused for a long moment. "I know we don't know who to trust in our own ranks, but these guys I handpicked myself. I go way back with them."

"Okay. Just making sure."

"I understand, man. Look, I'm right in the middle of sorting through all the shit we seized from the senator's office and residence. I flew out to his home in Virginia and found some stuff in his safe. Why don't you come over and have a look? I have a man there to drive you over."

"I hate to leave her," Manuel said quietly.

"I know. But Manny, you're going to be in for a long vigil. Come over here. I'll order some takeout, we can go through these computer files and you can get some rest. I have a guard detail on the senator so he's not going anywhere."

Manuel sighed. "All right."

He hung up then pinned the agents with his stare. "No one is allowed in that room except medical personnel."

Agent Redding nodded, his eyes softening with sympathy. Manuel wondered just what Tony had told the agents about his relationship with Jules.

With one last look in Jules's direction, Manuel walked toward the nurse's desk. He wrote his number down on a piece of paper and handed it to the same nurse who'd escorted him in to see Jules.

"If her condition changes or if she wakes up, call me immediately. Please."

The nurse smiled. "I will."

Manuel walked out of the unit, glancing back to see the two agents standing on either side of Jules's cubicle. He was met in the hall by yet another agent, who flashed ID at him.

"I'm supposed to take you to Tony's," the agent said.

Manuel sighed. "Yeah, Tony told me." And in truth, he wasn't in any shape to drive, so he nodded and followed the agent out of the hospital.

The afternoon sun blinded him as they walked through the parking lot. The agent gestured toward the Ford Expedition parked a few spaces away.

Manuel slid in as the agent started the vehicle, and soon they were winging their way through the Washington streets. He closed his eyes and leaned his head against the headrest. He couldn't get the image of Jules lying so helpless in the hospital bed out of his mind. The only spark of life he'd seen was the zigzag line flashing across the heart monitor. His only reassurance that she was alive.

A few minutes later, the SUV pulled to a stop, and Manuel opened his eyes. He mumbled his thanks to the agent who'd driven him then climbed out of the vehicle.

He strode up to Tony's door and knocked once before opening it. He found Tony in his office, surrounded by two laptops and a desktop computer, stacks of files and papers and other assorted boxes.

"Hey, man," Tony said in greeting. "How are you?"

Manuel shrugged. "Fine, I guess."

Tony grimaced in sympathy. "She'll make it, Manuel. She's a tough girl."

"What did you find?" Manuel didn't want to delve too deeply into a conversation about Jules. It was all he could do to maintain his composure as it was.

Tony gestured toward the computers. "The senator is up to his neck. I hacked into his secure files and found a list of all the hits he's personally ordered over the last twenty years. Including Jules's parents."

Pain stabbed him in the gut. "You mean Mom and Pop?"

"No, her real parents. Apparently Jules was to have been included in the hit. What I don't know is if the Pinsons somehow dropped Jules off in order to keep her safe or if Jules survived the hit and someone else dropped her in Tennessee where the Trehans lived."

"Who killed Mom and Pop?" Manuel asked. "Was it Sanderson?"

Tony nodded.

"Son of a bitch."

"The senator decided it would be more beneficial to him if he shut the NFR down. He planned to launch a sting operation against his own creation and take down the network and Sanderson with it. He had greater ambitions than just being the Director of Homeland Security. He planned to use the position as a launch pad for a presidential bid. His platform? Tough on terrorism. He would have been a shoe-in with the removal of the NFR as a threat."

"I take it Sanderson didn't like the idea."

Tony shook his head. "He wanted to use Jules to kill the senator. There were several reasons. One, with the senator gone, Sanderson would take over the NFR and continue operations as usual. As twisted as it sounds, Sanderson considered himself a solid patriot and the NFR, in his opinion, upheld the ideals and interests of the U.S."

Manuel clenched his fist. Patriot, his ass. The bastard had played him and Jules from the very beginning. Worse, he'd taken advantage of an innocent girl and turned her into a cold-blooded killer.

"Two," Tony continued, "after killing the Trehans, Sanderson knew he'd have leverage to make Jules do just about anything. That leverage was you. Here was a girl who only had one person left in the world who meant anything to her.

"And three, Sanderson realized some of the other operatives might balk at killing a U.S. senator. Sanderson counted on Jules's hatred of what the senator had done to her to make her carry out her mission."

Manuel's jaw tightened in rage. "He raped her."

Tony nodded, his expression grim. "The bastard kept a detailed journal in his safe. Recruiting Jules was personal. Payback for her parents deserting the cause. He also wanted to keep very close tabs on her. He was afraid of what she might know, what her parents might have somehow passed down to her. Apparently the Pinsons planned to blow the NFR wide open, taking the senator with it.

"Jules disappeared from the NFR for a time. Just before she surfaced in Colorado. I think that scared the senator. He ordered her killed. Only Sanderson was interested in keeping her alive so she could complete her mission. Basically she was caught in the middle of a huge power struggle. The senator wanted her dead, and Sanderson wanted her back in. Sanderson killed the Trehans to force her hand."

"Using me as bait," Manuel said, his voice shaking.

Tony nodded.

Manuel pounded his fist on the chair. "How far does this go up, Tony? How far is the CIA into this? Is our whole agency up to their necks in it?"

Tony handed him a piece of paper. "Names of those involved in the NFR's operations, either having knowledge of the group or having direct participation in the operations. The FBI is out making arrests now."

Manuel scanned the list, his stomach knotting as he passed over familiar names. His entire career at the CIA had been a facade. His only purpose was to be a puppet to dangle in front of Jules. Any good he'd thought he'd done evaporated under what his presence had accomplished for Jules. And the Trehans.

He didn't think he could become any more disillusioned than when he'd discovered Jules had lied to him. He was wrong.

"Why don't you get some rest, Manuel."

Manuel looked up to see his partner staring at him, his expression one of regret.

"Yeah, I think I will," he muttered, standing up from his chair.

"I've got some more hacking to do. The FBI wants a solid case against the senator before they march down to the hospital and arrest him."

Manuel nodded and trudged toward the spare bedroom. He didn't care what happened to the senator or the CIA. Not anymore. The only thing he cared about was lying in a hospital bed ten miles away fighting for her life.

Chapter Thirty

Jules floated in a sea of pain. She could hear voices, hushed tones, but they seemed miles away. She tried to open her eyes, but it felt as though someone had taped her eyelids shut.

What had happened to her? There wasn't a part of her that didn't hurt. Her throat felt sore and swollen, and her chest burned like the fires of hell.

She concentrated on the fuzzy images burning through her brain. The senator. He'd shot her. Manny's voice. She'd aimed at the senator. Had she fired? She didn't remember. Was she even alive?

Again she tried to open her eyes then whimpered in pain as a shard of light pierced her skull.

"Jules! Jules! Can you hear me?"

Was that Manny? Why couldn't she see anything? She blinked a few times, trying to draw focus.

"Squeeze my hand, baby. Squeeze it if you can hear me."

She didn't know where her hand was. For that matter, where were her feet? All she could feel was her chest. Pain consumed her.

A hand, Manny's hand, brushed across her palm. She latched onto it with all the strength she possessed, but only felt a flickering of movement in response.

"That's it, baby."

She could hear the excitement in his voice. Shouldn't he hate her? Why was he here? And where was here? But hearing his voice was such sweet relief. He was alive. But what of the senator? And Northstar. He was out there.

A few more blinks and she managed to make out Manny's large form standing over her. The room came into focus. She was in the hospital. Again.

"Jules?"

There was such relief on his face. She could make out the barest rim of moisture pooling in his eyes.

Tears stung her own eyes. He was here. He hadn't left her.

"Oh baby, don't cry. Do you hurt?"

She felt him leave the bed for a moment, then he returned with a woman. The nurse?

"Ms. Trehan, can you hear me?"

The nurse's voice was quiet and soothing. Jules tried to nod and pain lanced down her spine.

"You're in the hospital." The nurse smoothed a hand across Jules's brow. "You've been in ICU for two days now. Do you remember any of it?"

Two days? Hadn't it been a few minutes ago? She wasn't sure she remembered anything. She opened her mouth to speak, but nothing came out.

"Don't try to talk," the nurse said. "You were on a respirator until a few hours ago. Your throat will be sore."

The nurse's cool hand rested on Jules's. "I'll get you something for pain, would you like that?"

Jules squeezed.

"I'll be right back."

The nurse spoke to Manny, and the two of them conversed in low tones. Soon the nurse was back. A few minutes later, Jules gave herself over to the medication. She felt Manny's hand wrap around hers, and she gripped it tight, not wanting him to leave.

He must have sensed her fear. "I'm right here, Jules. I'm not going anywhere."

She relaxed and floated off, allowing herself to drift painlessly into oblivion.

Manuel stepped off the elevator, his hands clenched at his sides. He looked down the long hallway, his gaze flitting over the two agents posted outside the senator's hospital room.

With no hesitation, he strode forward until he was a few feet from the doorway. The agents came to attention.

"Sorry, Ramirez, we can't let you in there. You know that."

Manuel eyed the agent, saw the regret in his eyes. "I just want to have a *word* with the senator."

The agent stared at him for a long moment then stepped aside. "He better not have a mark on him when you're done. I'll give you five minutes. Then you're out of here."

Manuel nodded and shoved through the door. The senator lay propped up in his bed, a bandage around his right shoulder. He looked up warily when Manuel closed the door behind him.

Manuel didn't say anything. He pinned the senator with his stare until the older man shifted uncomfortably in the bed.

"What do you want?" he demanded.

"You better hope they lock you up in the deepest, darkest hole they can find," Manuel said, his voice deadly quiet. "Because if you ever see the light of day again, I'll hunt you down like the animal you are."

The senator paled then began to bluster. "You can't threaten me! I'm a United States senator."

"You'll be a *dead* U.S. senator if I ever find you," Manuel vowed. "I know what you did to Jules, and so help me if there weren't two federal agents standing outside your door, I'd kill you with my bare hands, right here, right now."

The senator's eyes shone with fear. "Get out," he said hoarsely. He yanked a finger toward the door. "Get out!"

"Rot in hell." Manuel turned and walked out the door, banging it behind him.

He strode back to the elevator, rode it to Jules's floor and settled into the chair beside her bed. He wasn't moving until she woke up.

For three days after Jules first regained consciousness, Manuel watched her drift in and out. Each time she stayed awake a little longer, but she hadn't spoken. She was in a lot of pain, and the medical personnel kept her heavily medicated. Manuel didn't leave her side. The hospital staff had long since stopped trying to make him leave.

On the fourth day, he'd fallen asleep in his chair when he heard the sweetest sound from Jules's bed. She spoke.

"Manny?"

It was the faintest whisper, shaky, a thread of pain woven in, but she said his name.

He jumped forward, scrambling out of his chair.

"I'm here."

"Can I have something to drink?" she rasped.

"I'll ask the nurse," he said as he pushed the call button.

A few seconds later, a nurse bustled in.

"So our patient's awake and talking? That's terrific."

"She wants something to drink," Manuel said.

The nurse poked and prodded for a few moments, listened to Jules's heartbeat and checked her bandages. "No reason she can't have a few sips of water. I'll notify the doctor of her condition."

As the nurse left the room, Manuel poured water into a cup then walked to Jules's bedside and put an arm behind her head. Gently, he eased her forward and put the drink to her lips.

She swallowed the liquid then slumped back in the bed. He set the cup by the sink and turned his attention back to her.

"How are you feeling?"

She turned blue eyes full of emotion on him. "I'm sorry, Manny. I know you hate me."

He felt like someone punched him in the stomach. "No, baby. No, I don't hate you."

He cupped her face in his palm, ran his fingers over her jaw.

"I lied to you," she whispered. "How can you not hate me, when I hate myself?"

A knot swelled in his throat. "I know everything, Jules. I know what the NFR is, what Northstar and the senator did to you. I know they used me to control you for the last three years, and I know you did what you did to protect me."

A tear trickled down her cheek. "The senator? Is he dead?"

"No, baby. He's not. But Northstar is."

She gasped in surprise. "Northstar's dead? But how? I mean, how do you know who he is?"

"He was my superior."

She grimaced but didn't look surprised by his announcement.

"I'll explain everything when you're feeling better. The important thing is that you're safe, Jules. No one can hurt you now. It's over."

She stared at him, suspicion clouding her expression. "Over?"

He nodded. "The senator was arrested. There's enough evidence to put him behind bars for the rest of his life."

More tears spilled down her cheeks. He smudged them with his thumb, caressed her face with his hand.

"I love you, Jules. I'm never letting you go again. We're free to have a life together. We can start over."

Jules drew in her breath and hiccupped as it caught in her throat. Manny didn't hate her. He wanted to be with her after all she'd done. It was more than she could have ever hoped for.

"I love you," she whispered.

"Get better, baby. You and I have a lot of time to make up for, and I plan to make the most of every minute."

An enormous weight lifted off her chest. Her heart took flight, lifted and soared. She was free. For the first time in three years, she was free.

Manny gathered her gently in his arms and pressed a kiss to the top of her head. "Go to sleep, baby. Nothing can hurt you anymore."

She pillowed her head on his chest, felt her tears soak into his shirt. Happy tears. For once, she didn't loathe her show of weakness. The man who held her made her strong.

Chapter Thirty-One

"Today's the day," Manny said as he rolled a wheelchair into her room.

Jules looked up from the bed, nervous excitement surging through her veins. It had been three weeks since she'd lain at death's door. Three weeks of lying in a hospital bed while Manny fussed endlessly over her. She was ready to be out.

He helped her into the wheelchair then checked the bandages over her chest. Other than a bit of soreness, the wound had healed marvelously.

"All set?" he asked.

At her nod, he pushed the wheelchair into the hallway.

"We'll stop by the nurses' station so they can give you your discharge instructions, then we'll be on our way."

She smiled. He sounded so cheerful. The worry that had been so firmly etched on his face for so long had disappeared. She could almost see the old Manny, the one she'd fallen in love with as a teenager.

"You know, I can walk just fine," she said as he pushed her toward the elevator.

"Hush. You'll have plenty of time for walking. For now, you'll take it easy."

She shook her head. He was enjoying this far too much.

They rode down on the elevator, then he pushed her toward the front entrance. She could see an SUV parked in the semicircular patient drop-off area through the automatic glass doors to the hospital.

They wheeled past the gift shop, and as he reached the doors, he slowed.

"Can you walk from here? The truck is just outside."

"Isn't that what I just said?" she asked dryly.

He grinned and leaned down to help her up. Despite her protests that she could walk, she still felt weak and was glad for his assistance.

The automatic doors swooshed open, and two men walked toward her and Manny. If they weren't government agents of some type, she'd eat every one of her bandages.

Her heart began to pound and her stomach coiled into a knot. Manny's arm tightened around her shoulders.

The men pulled out their badges. FBI agents.

"Jules Trehan, we'll have to ask you to come with us."

"The hell she will," Manny exploded. "She just got out of the hospital!"

One of the agents put up his hand in a placating manner. "Look, Ramirez, we aren't going to hurt her. We're just following orders."

Jules looked past the two agents to see two more entering the building. Sweat broke out on her forehead and she began to shake.

"Goddamn it, this isn't the time. Whose orders are you acting under?" Manny demanded. "She's in no shape for this."

"Am I being arrested?" she managed to get out. She had known this day was coming. The day when she would have to atone for her sins.

The second agent stepped forward and put his hand out toward Jules.

"If you so much as touch her, I'll kill you," Manny vowed.

The agent stepped back, and the two behind him advanced. This was quickly getting out of control.

She turned to Manny. "I have to go, Manny. You'll come with me." She wanted him to calm down before he went ballistic.

"I'm afraid that's not possible, Ms. Trehan. Our orders are to bring you in. Alone. Now if you'll follow me."

She swallowed back her panic and looked between Manny and the agents. Why were they taking her away from Manny?

Manny carefully shoved her behind him, providing a barrier between her and the agents. She peeked from behind his arm, needing to see what transpired.

"I want to talk to whoever's in charge. She's not going anywhere until I do," Manny said.

The agent sighed. Behind him, the other two agents drew their guns. "Ramirez, I know this sucks. We don't like it any more than you do, trust me. But our orders are to take her into protective custody. We'll take care of her, I promise."

"If you think I'm just going to let you walk in here and take her away without me, you're nuts."

"Don't make us force the issue."

Jules buried her face into Manny's back for a long second. Would she see him again? Or would they throw the book at her and more? Whatever the case, she wasn't a coward.

She stepped around him before he could pull her back and bravely faced her fate. "I'm ready."

Manny reached for her arm. "Jules, no! You don't have to go."

She looked up at him, tears filling her eyes. "You know what I've done, Manny. You can't have thought they wouldn't care."

"If you'll come with me, Ms. Trehan," the first agent said gently.

As soon as he put his hand on her arm, Manny exploded. The other three agents converged on him, pulling him away. In the end, it took their combined efforts and that of the hospital security guard to contain him.

Jules shook, her strength waning. Her knees threatened to buckle as she watched them pull Manny to the ground. The agent standing next to her put an arm around her to steady her.

"Not going to cuff me?" she asked.

"Whatever you may think, Ms. Trehan, I don't like this any more than Ramirez does. No, I'm not going to cuff you. You're recovering from serious injuries. We're going to be damn careful with you. Now let's go before Ramirez kills one of my men."

He put a firm arm around her and guided her toward the entrance.

"Jules!" Manny cried.

She turned to see one of the agents cuffing Manny in an effort to subdue him. He was wild beneath them, trying to reach her.

"I'll come for you, Jules. I won't let them get away with this. I swear it."

"I love you," she whispered, then allowed herself to be led away.

True to their word, the agents were very solicitous. She was escorted into a plush office and given a comfortable place to sit. She was asked if she was in pain or if she needed anything.

She needed Manny. The one thing they weren't going to give her.

She sat in the chair, tense, agonizing over her fate. She was a *terrorist*. No way they were going to let her walk away.

Several minutes later, the agent who'd escorted her in entered the room with another man.

"I'm sorry I didn't get around to introductions. I was a little concerned with what Ramirez might do," the agent said. "My name is Agent Vasquez, special agent in charge of the ongoing investigation into the NFR and its connection to the CIA, and to Senator Denison." He gestured toward the man standing next to him. "This is Senator Charles Whiting. He's heading the Senate Investigation Committee."

"Am I being arrested?" she asked again.

"No, Ms. Trehan, you are officially under protective custody," Agent Vasquez replied. "That is until we determine your role in the NFR."

"Why wasn't Manny allowed to accompany me?"

"Because he's a CIA agent, and the CIA is under heavy investigation at the moment. You won't be allowed any contact with him until the hearings are over."

"Hearings?"

Agent Vasquez turned to Senator Whiting, and the senator cleared his throat.

"The Senate is conducting a thorough investigation of its own, in addition to any ongoing FBI investigation. We'd appreciate your cooperation, of course."

Her eyes narrowed. "Of course."

The senator took the seat across from the couch she sat on. "I'll level with you, Ms. Trehan. Other than the documents we've recovered, and the computer files, you're our star witness. Your testimony is necessary if we want to successfully prosecute Senator Denison and the other twenty individuals involved in the NFR."

She cocked her head to the side. "I don't understand. Aren't there others who could testify? What of the other assas— agents?"

"The fact is, your position in the NFR is quite unique, Ms. Trehan. Everyone else was there of their own accord. They signed on knowing full well the range and scope of the group. You were different. It is that unique perspective which we wish to gain. You could provide us very valuable information."

"I see. And what can I expect in return?" She knew full well this was a bargaining session.

The senator's face hardened. "If you cooperate, we'll take into consideration the fact you were forcibly recruited and act accordingly. If you refuse, you'll be charged with acts of terrorism and stand trial with the others."

"I don't see that I have any choice," she said tightly.

The senator's eyes glinted in satisfaction. "I knew we could count on you, Ms. Trehan. Agent Vasquez here will see to your needs until your testimony."

"How long before I testify?"

"A few weeks at the most. You'll speak before a closed panel. It's vital that none of this is leaked to the press. Not until we have a firm idea of what we're dealing with and have acted to ensure all members of the NFR are captured."

She heard the warning in his voice and nodded.

"Very good, Ms. Trehan. I'll see you at the hearings then."
He gave her a curt nod and turned and left the room.

She glanced up at Agent Vasquez. "What now?"

Regret glimmered in his eyes. "I'm to take you to an
undisclosed location where you'll remain under protective
custody until your testimony."

"What does that mean, exactly?"

He sat down on the couch beside her and rubbed his hands
over his pants. "It means you'll go underground. Completely.
We'll provide a doctor to examine you on a daily basis and
provide all the medical attention you need. You won't see or talk
to anyone until you testify."

Her mouth popped open in shock. "I won't see Manny?"

Agent Vasquez shook his head. "I'm sorry."

She looked down at her hands and tried valiantly to
compose herself. Then she looked back up at the agent. "Can
you at least tell him what's happening?"

Vasquez sighed. "I'm not supposed to, but I'll let him know
something. I promise. He's probably already torn down the
damn FBI building demanding answers."

Jules smiled. Yes, he probably had. Her smile faded. What
would happen to her? Would she ever see Manny again? She
didn't trust the government as far as she could throw it. She
knew if they wanted, they could make her disappear, make it so
she'd never existed.

"I read your file, Ms. Trehan," Vasquez said quietly. "I know
how difficult this must be for you. I promise to do everything in
my power to make sure we hold up our end of the bargain."

"Thank you." She held up her hands in a gesture of
surrender. "I suppose we should go wherever it is you're
stowing me."

He nodded and helped her to her feet.

As Jules walked from the offices, she realized she didn't even know how to contact Manny once this was all over with.

Chapter Thirty-Two

"I don't give a rat's ass whether I'm supposed to be there or not," Manuel raged. "Nothing this side of a grenade is going to keep me out of those hearings."

Tony held up his hands. "Calm down, man. I'm working on it, I swear."

"Three weeks, Tony. *Three goddamn weeks* they've kept me from her!"

Manuel paced back and forth in front of Tony's desk, his agitation increasing with each second. He stopped and whirled around to rant some more.

"She was just released from the hospital. She was in no shape to be harangued and threatened into testifying. I have no idea how she is, if she's hurting, or how they're treating her, damn it."

"Manuel, you're going to blow a gasket or have an aneurysm if you don't calm down. They've provided her excellent medical care."

Manuel pounded Tony's desk with his fist. He wanted to kill someone. Preferably the sons of bitches who'd taken Jules and wouldn't let him see her.

"You get me into that hearing, Tony. I swear if you don't, you're going to be reading about me in tomorrow's paper."

"Listen to me, Manuel." Tony leaned forward and pinned Manuel with a determined stare. "Don't screw up now. Not when you're this close. I know how tough this has been for you. I've watched you prowl around like a caged lion for the last three weeks, but damn it, don't blow it when you're nearly there."

Fury consumed Manuel. Had consumed him since the bastards had taken Jules away. Worse was the fact he had no idea what was going on with her. He had no idea what their plans were. Surely they couldn't be planning to prosecute her.

He sat down on the other side of the desk from Tony and blew out an irritated breath. He leaned forward and rested his elbows on the polished wood. "Listen to me, Tony. I don't know what they're planning, but I won't let them lock her up for something she had no control over."

An uneasy look flickered across Tony's face.

"I don't like the way you just said that, Manuel."

"I just wanted you to know. If this all goes terribly wrong, I'm prepared to do whatever necessary to free Jules. Then we're going as far as we can. Someplace those bastards can't find us."

Tony swore. "Don't go flying off the handle, Manuel. You don't know what their plans are. Chances are they just want her testimony."

"That's just it, Tony. We don't know what their plans are. The bastards could have told us. They left us with our balls twisting in the wind."

Tony rubbed a tired hand over his face, and Manuel felt a pang of regret. All this had been hard on Tony, too, and his partner had spent a lot of sleepless nights sewing up the case against Denison. Tony had personally combed through each and every computer file, personal document and telephone record of Sanderson and the senator.

"I know you love her, man. Hell, maybe I'd do the same if the woman I loved was facing a damn Senate Investigation Hearing."

Tony leaned back and stared at the ceiling.

"I tell you what. I'll call in a favor. Senator Bilkins's secretary owes me. I'll see if she can get you into the hearing."

Manuel raised his brow. "Secretary?"

Tony held out a hand. "Don't ask."

"Thanks, man. I owe you, yet again."

Tony shook his head. "Screw that. You'd do the same for me. I just want things to work out for you and Jules. That girl deserves a break."

Tony picked up the phone and dialed a number. After several minutes of sweet talking, plus one promise of dinner, he hung up and rolled his eyes.

"Okay, man, you're in. She's sending over the badge you'll need to get into the hearing by courier. Should be here within the hour."

Manuel reached over the desk and hauled Tony into a hug.

"Ah hell, man, knock that shit off."

"Thanks, Tony. We'll name our firstborn after you."

Tony grinned. "I'll hold you to that."

Jules sat stiffly at the small table before a panel of ten senators. They'd asked her questions for three hours. She was exhausted both mentally and physically. They'd left no stone unturned in their investigation.

She'd refused counsel. She was guilty as hell. They knew it, and she knew it. Nothing a lawyer could do for her would change that fact.

Every single detail from the past three years of her life was now entered into record. She'd answered their questions with bloodless lips, her fingers curled tightly into balls.

She flinched at some of the things that spilled from her mouth. And still they questioned her. Prodded. Poked until she felt she had no more blood to bleed.

She slumped forward in her chair, fatigue overwhelming her. Would the day never end? How many more times could she relive the horrible events of her past?

Finally Senator Whiting leaned forward and spoke into the microphone. "You've been very cooperative, Ms. Trehan. I know I speak for all of my colleagues when I say your testimony was very helpful. Your honesty was appreciated."

He exchanged glances with the other senators then leaned forward once more.

"In light of your testimony, and the countless documents and files that support your claims, we feel it would be a crime to prosecute you for your involvement."

He paused and his expression softened.

"You're free to go, Ms. Trehan. With our thanks."

She sat there numbly, looking at him in disbelief. Could that really be the end of it? Finally? She was free to go?

Beside her, Agent Vasquez put an arm around her shoulders and helped her up. She looked at him, too, her lips trying to form the question.

"It's over," he said quietly.

She swayed precariously. Vasquez caught her before she fell and guided her toward the door. Once outside, she broke away and hurried for the bathroom. There, she leaned over a toilet and emptied the contents of her stomach.

She stood, braced against the toilet until her stomach stopped rolling. Slowly, she straightened and walked to the sink to rinse her mouth. Her reflection startled her. She looked like hell.

When she rejoined Vasquez in the hall, he looked at her in concern.

"Everything all right?" he asked as he took her arm.

She nodded.

They walked slowly down the long hall leading out to the main entrance. As they walked, Jules's mind whirled. She had to find Manny. She looked up at Vasquez, knowing how stupid her request was going to sound.

"Agent Vasquez, do you...that is, do you know how I can get in touch with Manny Ramirez?"

She felt stupid for asking, but she didn't even know where Manny lived.

A peculiar smile flashed across Vasquez's face.

"I think I do, Ms. Trehan."

He gestured toward the door. Jules looked up to see Manny standing there. Her heart tumbled and fell. She stopped in her tracks. Had he been at the hearing? Had he heard her testimony? The thought made her want to vomit all over again.

She curled and uncurled her fingers and tamped back the urge to flee from his scrutiny.

Then he simply opened his arms.

Tears flooded her eyes, and she flew across the room, launching herself at him.

He gathered her tightly against him. She buried her face in his neck and sobbed.

"Ah, baby, it's okay. Don't cry," he soothed, stroking her hair.

Manuel glanced over Jules's head at Agent Vasquez, who stared at them with something akin to satisfaction.

"Thank you," Manuel said sincerely. "Thank you for looking out for her."

Vasquez nodded. "You're welcome. It was my pleasure. You take good care of this little lady."

"I'm never letting her go again," Manuel vowed.

The agent smiled and walked away, leaving Manuel and Jules alone.

Manuel hugged Jules to him and closed his eyes, enjoying the sensation of her in his arms. He'd never felt such relief as when the Senate committee dismissed her. Watching the torture they'd put her through had damn near killed him.

He pulled her away from him and ran his eyes hungrily across her face. She was pale, her eyes rimmed with fatigue and pain, but she was beautiful. So very beautiful.

He bent his head and captured her lips in a long, delicious kiss. Then he hugged her to him again, just wanting to feel her against his chest.

"I missed you."

She started crying again, and it tore at his soul.

"Come on, let's get out of here."

Without caring what anyone watching thought, he picked her up and cradled her in his arms.

"Were you there?" she asked in a low voice.

He nodded. "I wouldn't have missed it."

She hung her head in shame, and anger coursed over his body. He set her down in the parking lot next to his SUV, then he tilted her chin up so she looked him in the face.

"I love you, Jules," he said fiercely. "Do you honestly think hearing the hell you went through for the last three years changed that? God, I wanted to howl, I wanted to cry, I wanted to kill the bastards for what they did to you, but never, *never* did I think any less of you."

She stared up at him. "Do you mean that?"

"Baby, if I was any more serious, I'd be lying in the hospital with a heart attack."

"I love you so much," she whispered.

"Marry me, Jules. Marry me, spend the rest of your life with me, have my babies, the picket fence, the whole nine yards."

A glorious smile spread across her face. It was as though a ray of sunshine spilled across a frozen pond.

"Yes. Oh, yes."

He fused his lips to hers once more. She curled her arms around his neck, and he anchored her body to him.

"There's just one thing," he said in between kisses.

"What's that?"

"I sort of promised Tony we'd name our firstborn after him."

She laughed, and he felt a thrill all the way down to his toes. She had such a beautiful laugh, and it had been so long since he'd seen her so full of joy.

"I'm home," she said in an aching voice. "I'm finally home."

"Yes, baby, you are. And I've been waiting for you all along."

About the Author

New York Times and USA Today bestselling author Maya Banks lives in Texas with her husband, three children and assortment of cats. When she's not writing, she can be found hunting, fishing or playing poker. A southern girl born and bred, Maya loves life below the Mason Dixon, and more importantly, loves bringing southern characters and settings to life in her stories.

Check Maya's website out at: www.mayabanks.com

Email Maya: maya@mayabanks.com

Find Maya on Facebook:

www.facebook.com/pages/Maya-Banks/323801453301?ref=ts

Or follow Maya on Twitter: twitter.com/maya_banks

One woman's mission to bring down a sexy elemental shifter turns into a battle of wills...and hearts.

Into the Mist

© *2008 Maya Banks*

Falcon Mercenary Group, Book 1

Hostage recovery specialist Eli Chance has a secret. He was born a shifter. A freak of nature.

While on a mission, Eli's men and their mercenary guide are exposed to a powerful chemical agent, and suddenly his secret has become easier to hide. Now he's not the only one with the gift. But for his men, this "gift" is becoming more and more of a curse.

Tyana Berezovsky's brother Damiano was the guide for Eli's team and was the worst affected by the chemical. As he grows increasingly unstable, Tyana fears she's going to lose him to the beast he is becoming.

Tyana will do whatever it takes to help him, even if it means using her body to go after the one man she thinks holds all the blame—and possibly the cure. Eli Chance.

Warning: Violence, blood, guns, knives, ass kicking, people who do mean things, bad people dying, explicit sex and smart mouths.

Available now in ebook from Samhain Publishing.

Enjoy the following excerpt from Into the Mist...

And so it began.

Eli bit out a curse as one of the silent alarms was triggered. Though he'd been expecting company, he hadn't expected it so soon.

She certainly could have picked a better time. One when both Ian and Braden weren't off prowling the grounds looking for kitty food.

Then again, he might do well to be more worried about them than Tyana Berezovsky. She might shoot first and ask questions later.

Gabe was God knows where, having decided yesterday to disappear into the village down the mountain, probably in search of pussy. His parting words had been something to the effect that since Eli was so keen for Tyana to find his ass then he could deal with her when she got here.

Good help was hard to find and harder to keep.

None of the others seem to think Tyana posed any sort of threat. Eli knew better. To them she was just a woman. Easily handled, easily subdued.

He smiled. He was looking forward to the challenge.

Pulling his hair behind his neck, he secured it with a leather tie then reached for his shoes and tugged them on. He might as well either go save her from the cats or save the cats from her. One way or another, someone better damn well be grateful.

A quick glance of the infrared monitor told him she was slowly making her way toward the south entrance. The most obvious course would just be to meet her, but where would the fun be in that?

No, he was going to enjoy this. Savor it. He smiled again. And maybe before the night was over, he'd take the impending confrontation to the bedroom.

He stepped into the night and breathed deep of the chilly air. Quietly he slipped beyond the shadows cast by the glow of the interior lights. He went east, cutting a direct path to intercept her...from behind.

He closed his eyes and let go, embraced the faint mist, let it curl around him, and then he became the very air he breathed.

A faint breeze carried him through the trees. Ahead, he saw movement. He looked down as he floated above the figure clad in black.

She moved with grace and stealth, her movements slow and calculated. She made no noise, left no disturbance in her wake.

He contented himself with watching her, gauging her patterns as she stopped and patiently observed the area around her. He saw her shiver then look quickly back, and he wondered if she'd sensed him again.

He ventured closer, wrapping around her hair and whispering softly against the nape of her neck. A slight shift in the air alerted him to her movement. Silver glinted in moonlight as a knife appeared in her hand. With the other, she grasped the barrel of her rifle and hauled it over her shoulder to cradle in front of her.

A faint apparition, he wrapped himself around her in a veil of mist, faint trails of smoke curling around her wrists. Then he jolted back to his human form, his fingers like bands around her small bones.

She exploded in a flurry of motion. He went sailing over her shoulder and wondered again how the hell she always managed to get the drop on him no matter how prepared he was. He was starting to take it personally.

There was the wee little matter that he honestly wasn't trying to hurt her, but still. He could have simply slit her throat, and he consoled himself with the fact that if he was a real bastard, he could have broken her neck.

But no, instead he was lying on the ground feeling like a goddamn sissy for being beaten up by a girl.

He started to pick himself up and found a boot pressed against his neck. He grabbed her ankle, yanked the knife out of the side sleeve then wrenched her back, making her fall.

They both bolted to their feet, knives in hand, and began circling.

"You're late," he said, though he wasn't about to admit he hadn't really expected her for a few more days.

"I had a few technical difficulties," she said, and it was then, when she turned her head and a sliver of moonlight hit her face that he could see her split lip.

"Piss off one too many people, my love?"

She bared her teeth. "The last man to piss me off died in a Paris alley. I wouldn't push my luck if I were you."

"Isn't that what you're here to do, though? Kill me?"

He watched intently for any change, any flicker, some sign of what was going round that pretty head of hers. That incredibly stubborn, obnoxious, gorgeous head of hers.

"I'm pretty sure we've had this conversation before," she said in a bored voice.

"Then what are you here for?"

He blinked, and she was in his face, her knee planted in his stomach and one fist buried in his ribs. He let out a growl of pain but didn't budge. Instead he yanked her against him. She gasped in surprise and the knife fell from her hand.

When she brought her other knee up, he blocked it with his.

"You're getting too predictable, love," he murmured. "You have a morbid fascination with a man's balls. Is that any way to treat such delicate equipment?"

She cursed in what sounded like four different languages. He recognized at least two and raised his eyebrows.

"And to think I've kissed that mouth."

Her eyes glittered in the moonlight. Just before she reared back and head butted him.

Pain exploded over him. He let go and stumbled back, holding his nose as blood gushed. Jesus H. Christ. Bitch was vicious!

She took off in a dead run. He watched her leap like a damn gazelle over rocks and roots and disappear into the night.

He vaporized into smoke and streamed after her.

He materialized in front of her this time, stopping her in her tracks. She let out a disgusted grunt.

"Can't beat the weak woman without resorting to your little smoke tricks?" she taunted.

He grinned and wiped more blood from his nose. "If you want me to apologize for pressing my advantage, you'll be waiting a long time. If you'd just play nice, I'd invite you in for a drink..." he made a slow up and down sweep of her body with his gaze, "...and maybe show you just how hospitable I can be."

"And you say *I* have an obsession with that part of the male anatomy."

"I'm a man. We think with our dicks, remember?"

She responded with a quick jab. He dodged and punched back, connecting with her shoulder. It wasn't enough to even knock her back, but he heard her quick intake of breath, and he frowned.

Then once again, he found himself staring up at the stars when she executed a lightning roundhouse kick to his jaw. And she was off again.

Damn but he must have it awfully bad for this chick to put this much effort into getting into her pants.

He got up, rubbing his jaw, and set off. She was making steady progress toward the house. What did she want? She wasn't trying to kill him. Hurt him? Taunt him? Yes. But she was pulling her punches every bit as much as he was, and she hadn't tried to filet him with the damn machete she called a knife.

Chasing after women wasn't his style, but damn if he wasn't wagging his ass after her like a damn lap dog. He had a sneaking suspicion the feisty little wench just might be his dream woman.

The constantly trying to do him bodily harm could put a serious kink in their relationship, though.

He shifted again and streaked after her, suddenly weary of the chase. It was time to end it. He wanted her. Wanted to taste her again. To get so deep inside her that he lost all sense of himself.

A low growl echoed across the night.

As he rounded the corner of the west wing of the house, he saw Tyana frozen, staring at two pacing cats.

Thirteen stories up. Two broken hearts. One last chance...

Shaken
© *2010 Dee Tenorio*

Surgeon Grant Sullivan's once-perfect life lies in ruins. His daughter is gone—lost in a tragic accident he dare not allow himself to remember—and his beautiful wife now stares at him from across a legal table, insisting she wants nothing from him.

Julia Sullivan lost everything, especially her illusions about her marriage, after the accident. Her grief only seemed to drive Grant further into his emotional shell—except for the nights he turned to her in silent, furious passion. Unable to live like a ghost in her old life, she's packed up what's left of her broken heart and is ready to move on. Alone.

Determined to break their stalemate, Grant follows Julia onto the elevator just in time for an earthquake. Trapped for hours in a building pressure cooker of unspoken pain, he'll do anything to remind her what she's leaving behind, as deliciously as he can. But giving her what she needs to save their marriage is the one thing that could destroy his soul.

Warning: Heartbreak and passion ahead—desperate doctor determined to save his marriage at any cost...except for the one secret his wife will do anything to uncover.

Available now in ebook from Samhain Publishing.

Enjoy the following excerpt from Shaken...

Julia leaned against the wall of the elevator car, watching her husband come ever closer, each step a slow, stalking movement. She could still taste him on her lips, knew what he planned to do if she let him close enough. The question was whether or not she wanted to.

No, that wasn't even a question.

Whether she *should.*

Her body shook, not in fear—she could never be afraid of Grant—but with need. That kiss ignited too many feelings, awakening something in her that had been blessedly numb since she'd left their home. Desire.

He stood almost over her now, their bodies nearly touching. His warmth called to her, his breath. If she wanted him, all she had to do was reach out and touch. Undo the buttons on that gray shirt, find the muscled flesh beneath. Then she'd be able to press her face to his skin, taste it with wet, sucking kisses that made him groan deep in his chest. Her fingers itched, ready to seek out the muscled ripples along his ribs.

She tightened them on the metal handrail instead.

This was why she'd left. Because Grant turned every quiet moment, every opportunity to talk, into sex. He disappeared from her emotionally, verbally, physically in every way except for the moments he was stripping her. Pleasuring her. Filling her until she screamed from the raw pleasure of it. And then he'd always leave her afterward. Leave her more alone with each experience, until she felt as if there were nothing left of her. She couldn't face it again.

"This is hardly the place for what you're thinking," she said, but the argument lacked the strength she knew it needed.

"This is the only place we have left, don't you think?" His fingertip touched her jaw, soft as a feather, tilting her face up to his. "Haven't you missed this, Julia?"

So much her body, her soul, ached day and night.

His lips grazed hers. "I feel like I'm breathing again for the first time in months." Firmer pressure...or had she lifted onto her toes to press closer? She wasn't sure. "Like my heart's beating again, just touching you."

Hers, too. Beating so fast it felt like a flutter.

His fingers left her jaw, the backs of them trailing down her neck to the collar of her blouse, which felt like it was strangling her. He tugged on the tie, gently. Asking permission. God, how she wanted to give it to him.

She stared up, his face so close to hers, but his gaze was on the tie at her neck. His black lashes spread like thick fans just above his stark cheekbones. So haggard, so...lost. She lifted her hand to his cheek, his heavy stubble tickling her palm. If she gave in, though, he'd be gone in a heartbeat...

It hit her then. Gone where? They were trapped. He couldn't walk away this time. Couldn't leave her behind. Couldn't hide from her questions. Her love.

Against all her better judgment, hope flared in her heart.

"Let me touch you, Jules," he whispered roughly, lowering his mouth to the corner of hers. Slowly he made his way down her body, touching but not taking. Almost as if he couldn't help himself. Until he knelt before her, hands on her thighs, waiting. Watching her. "Let me make it better."

God, did she have the strength? Could she take one more risk, after everything she'd already lost? Her daughter, her marriage... Could she bear it if she tried to reach for her husband and everything she feared about their relationship was true?

Could she bear it if she was wrong and never took the opportunity to find out for sure?

Closing her eyes, she finally let go of the rail. She reached blindly for his hands, guiding them to the hem of her skirt...and underneath. Her breath slipped out in a rush when he began lifting the fabric, sliding the skirt higher and higher up her thighs.

Her breath disappeared.